In Search of Diddly Squat

or: The Mall Walker's Guide to the Universe

RAY OLIVER

iUniverse, Inc.
New York   Bloomington

iUniverse books may be ordered through booksellers or by contacting:

iUniverse
1663 Liberty Drive
Bloomington, IN 47403
www.iuniverse.com
1-800-Authors (1-800-288-4677)

Because of the dynamic nature of the Internet, any Web addresses or links contained in this book may have changed since publication and may no longer be valid. The views expressed in this work are solely those of the author and do not necessarily reflect the views of the publisher, and the publisher hereby disclaims any responsibility for them.

ISBN: 978-1-4401-9584-6 (sc)
ISBN: 978-1-4401-9586-0 (ebook)
ISBN: 978-1-4401-9585-3 (dj)

Printed in the United States of America

iUniverse rev. date: 12/10/2009

To Jay – who brings (Camp) Sunshine to our lives –
and music to our hearts.

Acknowledgment:

Thanks to Sara Idzik – typist, betting buddy, and world class
colleague.

Special thanks to Katherine Oliver Birkbeck – the world's
greatest photographer and cover designer. Check out her work at
www.kbirkbeckphotography.

Chapter I. – Diddly Squat Or: Poor Sheryl

I like Sheryl Crow. What's not to like? She's pretty, smart, and talented. She writes songs, sings well, and plays the guitar, the bass guitar, and the piano. Once upon a time, she was a music teacher. Sure would have been fun being in her class.

And now, Sheryl Crow is the inspiration for an amazing book, one of those "must read" jobs that Oprah will, no doubt, endorse. It might even be considered a blockbuster, although no blocks were hurt or busted in the writing of it. And you, gentle reader, are currently reading it. I don't know where that "gentle reader" came from, I think I read a book that used it once, and I liked it so much I stole it. But it's okay if ungentle readers also read it – I'm all about inclusiveness.

It all began with Sheryl Crow's *Soak Up the Sun*. It's got a nice beat. If I were on *American Bandstand* I'd give it a 92. It you don't understand the reference to a treasured icon of Americana, you should:

a) Put down the book and go play in your sandbox
b) Find the nearest geezer and ask for clarification, or
c) Keep reading, since not understanding the reference will not change your life.

The point is, I like the song, but I do have a slight problem with the lyrics. Not all of them, just a few. I don't care about her friend, the Communist, who holds meetings in his RV. I don't care about her crummy job or her 45s, or anything except two lines. (Those were all specific song lyrics, in case you didn't guess that). Here's my problem:

I don't have digital
I don't have diddly squat.

I've skipped a few spaces here. I did so for absorption purposes. You know, so you could soak up the deep, philosophical message. I could skip a few more lines if necessary, but I'm confident that those still reading can see the problem.

Sheryl Crow does not have digital! Worse yet, she does not have diddly squat, and it appears that the poor girl wants both of those things.

I know that some would argue that it is not really Sheryl Crow speaking, just a fictional character she made up. To that totally logical, valid observation, I say...nothing. I actually have chosen to ignore logic and validity because it does not suit my purpose. I now feel like a politician. I may need a shower.

It is also possible that Diddly Squat was a pet nickname for Lance Armstrong. That would explain the angst but ruin the song.

Back to the point at hand, or elbow, or foot... Sheryl Crow does not have diddly squat, and I think we should help her. I'd like to suggest a celebrity golf tournament, or a telethon, or maybe an on-line auction to address this terrible inequality.

I don't have diddly squat, either. Who would have guessed that Sheryl and I have so much in common? (I decided that we are now on a first name basis because of our common lack of squat). Of course, I'm not exactly sure what diddly squat is, or what it looks like, or what I'd do with it if I found it. I've never really missed it, but that's not the point. If a pre-eminent musical master is moved to write about her lack of diddly squat, I'm moved, also.

Doesn't diddly squat sound like a person's name – or at least a character's name? Can't you visualize the animated adventures of Diddly Squat and his side-kick Numb Nuts? Or a children's series of books – *Diddly Squat and the Golden Compass, The Return of*

Diddly Squat, Diddly Squat Rides Again, and *Diddly Squat and the Lost Ark.*

I'll bet there are people whose last name is Squat. I was going to get out the Knoxville phone book – or directory if you are a high brow – and look it up. I'm a low brow, and that seemed like research, so I decided against it. I'll bet that raised a few eyebrows. Research is overrated and gets in the way of my pre-conceived ideas, so I avoid it. Now I feel like a talk radio host. I really do need a shower.

Anyway, in my mind, I visualize Mr. and Mrs. Squat. She probably had a wonderful last name, but she gave in to the archaic notion that only women have to change their names when they marry, so now she is a Squat. Eventually, Mrs. Squat becomes pregnant, is with child, had the rabbit die, got a bun in the oven, or got knocked up. It really makes one wonder who came up with all these delightful euphemisms, but there is Mrs. Squat, having her morning sickness every evening, and eventually she and her husband have to name this child.

Many readers are probably thinking, "Let me guess, he's going to suggest they name their child Diddly. How predictable."

Many readers would be wrong. They don't know Diddly. I was not going to suggest they name their child Diddly. That would be the middle name. I was going to suggest they name their child Bo.

Bo is a perfectly good name. It is gender neutral, hence Bo Derek and Bo Schembechler. Also, Bo Peep and Bo Bice. So the little bugger would be named Bo Diddly Squat, for those who need things spelled out. The nickname would be B.D., and if the parents didn't like him or her they could ship the child to Sheryl Crow, who would have all the Diddly Squat she could handle, and the world would be a happy place.

I'm glad I got this off my chest, although it was never really on my chest. That's just one of those dumb sayings we all repeat. I think I'll go soak up some sun. Or shower.

Chapter II. – Mall Walkers
Or: Duh

I am a high school teacher. That's another thing Sheryl and I have in common. Not the high school part, just the teacher part. But unlike Sheryl, I did not leave my precious students to seek fame and fortune. This is either because I am an extremely dedicated educator or because I have no talent. I'll let the readers judge that.

Every time someone discovers that I teach school they immediately want to know what it is that I teach. That's logical. Sometimes I tell them, "Nuclear quantum molecular biophysics," or some other nonsense. Actually, I've never done that because I'm not smart enough to think of that "on the spot." Off the spot, maybe, but not on the spot. But maybe the next time someone asks...

Usually I just go ahead and tell the truth. I know, it's amazing, but I do. I honestly tell them I teach English and creative writing. By the way, it ticks me off that English gets to be capitalized and creative writing does not. It's just one of those grammar rules. I'll bet the original grammar rules were made by people who never had sex. They just withered away in their unhappy existence and died virgins. Collectively, they were known as the Curmudgeon Virgins, or CVs for short. The cause of their curmudgeonness was. . . well. . . obvious, and that is why we have grammar rules that are about as helpful and useful as a childproof bottle cap in a senior citizen's center. I'll bet most readers, both gentle and ungentle, were not expecting this valuable lesson in grammatical history. You are welcome.

If there were a convention held in, let's say, Dubuque, Iowa, and the only criteria (or criterion to be exact) for attendance was that you had to be a mother-in-law, there might be numerous people in attendance. Okay, there would have to be lots of free food and drink, and George Clooney, Michael Phelps, David Beckham, and Johnny Depp would have to pole dance, but now there would be numerous people in attendance. One might say there would be lots of mother-in-laws there, but one would be in serious grammatical trouble, because the CVs decided that the correct plural is mothers-in-law, which doesn't even sound plural.

The major theme of this chapter is not the evils perpetuated by the Curmudgeon Virgins, however. It's about mall walkers.

When people ask me what I teach and I reply, "English," it's like they take two psychic steps backwards, as if I am contagious. Some promise to watch their grammar in front of me. Not beside me or behind me, but in front of me. Others feel compelled to tell me how English was their worst subject in school, or how much they hated it, or how they failed it. One even said, "I done well in my other subjects, but English were hard."

I nodded and tried to look sympathetic. I'm not sure what people expect me to say to that. "Sucks for you" sounds harsh. So does, "You don't actually vote or breed, do you?" So I mumble something and move on, knowing, absolutely knowing, that these are the people who "Don't like them foreigners who can't even speak good English."

Sometimes I think the best answer to what I really teach would be, "Logic." That's because I teach teen-agers, and teen-agers and logic are strangers. If you don't think so, try to teach hormone driven, lust-filled sixteen-year-olds the joys of *Julius Caesar*. By the way, the plural of sixteen-year-old is different than it is for mother-in-law. Shouldn't it be sixteens-year-old?

Math teachers spend their lives trying to solve for "x," while their students are struggling with their locker combinations. The quadratic formula pales when thoughts of sex, drugs, and rock and roll dominate the day.

I'm not one of those "kids today" people. I like teaching. I just know what's on their minds. It was on my mind in high school, too. It was probably on the Curmudgeon Virgins' minds, not that it did them any good.

Some adults are also hormonal, lust-driven maniacs. There is a word for those adults. That word is senator. I know -- some of you think that's ridiculous. Perhaps it is a bit narrow in scope. I will cave in to reader pressure and include mayor, governor, congressman, or, occasionally, president.

Which brings me to the mall walkers.

My teen-agers like to make fun of everything except themselves. One of their favorite targets, besides Mexicans, gay people, slow drivers, old slow drivers, people with mental or physical disabilities, teachers, parents, police, boy bands, girl bands, slutty people (called hos – no grammatical rules there) are mall walkers.

Go figure. Not literally – I don't want you solving for "x." Just think about the group battling the worst epidemic of teen-age obesity making fun of elderly people who are in shape.

They really seem annoyed by mall walkers, and I have yet to hear a logical explanation for this illogical resentment.

I'm actually surprised their paths have crossed. Mall walkers are usually early risers. Teen-agers think noon is the butt-crack of dawn. Yet there are my students, using mall walker as a put down.

Maybe they think they're sneaky – after all, they wear sneakers. Maybe they are annoyed because they got lapped by a seventy-year-old once. Maybe several seventies-year-old walked through the oh so cool clot of teen-agers cruisin' the mall lookin' to hook up with the first thing that moves and is not a mall walker. Who knows?

I'll bet store owners like mall walkers. I've never bothered to ask them, but you can do this the next time you're at the mall. I'll bet crime rates are lower in malls where people are exercising. I'm guessing there has been a 16.7 percent drop since mall walking began. In fact, from now on, I'm going to use that stat.

I wonder how mall walking began. I'd be very interested in the history of mall walking. Who was the first? What prompted him or her? Where did people walk in the B.M. days? (That's before malls, in case you were wondering.) I think Mall Walking 101 would be a wonderful college course.

I bet sales have increased as well. How many walkers stop in after completing their circuit to purchase something? An 11.4 percent increase in sales is what I'm saying. And I seem to be doing a lot of betting in this chapter, but only for recreational purposes.

Let's review. Mall walkers are in shape, which helps our medical costs. They deter crime. They help the economy. Clearly, here is a group that deserves far more respect than they are getting. I think I have a solution.

The problem is the name. Mall Walker, especially if it is capitalized, sounds like a first cousin of Street Walker. We need a name change. I like Public Perambulator myself – although it is a bit esoteric. Store Stalker doesn't quite do it, nor does Lobby Lizard. It needs to be loftier. Perhaps Untraditional Shopper would work. The initials would spell US – and their slogan would be, *Come Join US.*

Maybe we need a contest. Everyone should find Sheryl Crow's e-mail and send her suggestions for the new name. In the meantime...wait...I don't like meantime...I want the nicetime... In the nicetime, STOP DISRESPECTING THE BACKBONE OF AMERICA. Mall Walkers of the World UNITE!

Take that, teen-agers. And since you now know that I am a teacher, I feel a need to end this chapter with a test. Here it is:

The term Curmudgeon Virgin sounds like:
   a) The newest ship in the Norwegian cruise line fleet
   b) The name of a local rock band
   c) A serious medical condition, or
   d) The supreme court

The correct answer is whichever one you like. I'm an easy grader.

Chapter III. – The Sporting Life
Or: A Swill in Time

Is there anything more pathetic than America's love of sporting events? Grown men and women will spend untold hours and untold fortunes following their favorite teams and athletes. I wonder if there are any told hours and told fortunes. I guess if they were told we'd know the answer.

Any ball that can be kicked, thrown, passed, shot, dribbled, or caught will attract a crowd.

People will show up in droves to watch other people drive. (I think Droves is in Wisconsin, but I'm not sure). They'll watch people on skates armed with sticks. They'll watch people wearing very bad clothes hit a very small ball with very large clubs. Tennis, gymnastics, beach volleyball (especially the women, for some reason), swimming, diving, running, jumping – it doesn't matter. America loves sports – is addicted to sports – is obsessed and possessed and dominated by sports.

And that's why America is a great country. I am proud to be a part of the addiction – except for watching other people drive, which is like having a root canal, only longer and noisier. And fumier. And more uncomfortable.

Do I think teachers and baseball players should swap salaries? Yup. Should nurses and N.B.A. stars trade pay? Absolutely – as should firemen and policemen and so many others. Will it ever happen? No. Am I bitter? No. It's just the way it is.

The current stereotype of a sports fan is a couch potato who spends all day yelling at the T.V. while swilling beer. I resent such stereotyping. First of all, I – and millions of other patriots like me – am not a couch potato. In fact, during sporting events, I do not sit on the couch. I have a large, comfortable chair. My Chair. If that sounds Archie Bunkerish, so be it. (If you don't understand that reference, see the multiple-choice regarding *American Bandstand*). Sitting in My Chair (with its matching ottoman) is not the same as being a couch potato. The fact that the ottoman can serve as a punching bag at certain crucial moments is just one example of the differences. Actually, I don't view it as a punching bag. I prefer tension releaser, frustration elixir, or bad coaching decision compensator. With all this activity, plus game preparation, coaching, cheering, referee baiting, scoreboard watching, and various pools or wagers to keep track of (for entertainment purposes only, of course) this is far from being the sedentary activity "couch potato" implies.

And if I did sit on a couch, I would certainly not be a potato. How in the name of the NCAA did potato become the cliché of choice? Of all the possible fruits and vegetables, why pick the potato?

If I were an inactive participant, I'd be a carrot. It has alliteration going for it, and has the orange color we Tennessee fans prefer. I could even handle being a couch cucumber. Cucumbers have the "cool as a" reputation, and it is still alliterative. Couch kumquat has alliteration, but not much else.

Having successfully (in my not so humble opinion) exploded the couch potato part of the myth, I would like to address the beer swilling aspect. Once again, I hope this will point out the danger of perpetuating these ignorant stereotypes (not to be confused with intelligent stereotypes).

I – and millions of other patriots like me – do not swill beer. Ever. I drink beer. I imbibe. I indulge. I've been known to "down a few." Never "up a few" – always down. It is possible that, once or twice, I may have, during a particularly tense moment, even guzzled. It is amazing how many tense moments can occur during a game. But I have never swilled – not once. A man has to draw the line somewhere – I prefer the bathroom wall – and I draw the metaphorical line at swilling. Thou shalt not swill.

Actually, I believe I engage in libation lubrication and liquidation. In fact, I consider myself a libation lubrication and liquidation expert, and I need to add that to my resumé.

There is one troubling aspect to being a sportsaholic. Sometimes I become a person I would make fun of if I saw him in action. I am relieved that we cannot see ourselves.

In public, when I attend a sporting event, I am a well-mannered individual. I am the kind of fan you would love to sit next to. I'm a good sport. I don't drink at the event because I'm afraid I'll have to use the bathroom and miss the greatest play in a generation. Besides, I hate inebriated buffoons who ruin the contest for those around them.

But at home, in front of my big screen T.V., where there are no lines to the bathroom and a DVR at the ready, I am, occasionally, an idiot. If my wife were writing this, she might say occasionally is kind. She might opt for often, or frequently, or usually, or always. To which I would respond, "That's ridiculous. In my book, it's occasionally. If you disagree, write your own damn book."

Why am I so different at home than I am in public? I don't know – I may have to research this and get back to you. (Don't hold your breath). Wouldn't it be cool if you could hold your breath? I mean in your hands. Then you could have a breath ball fight. Wait – upon further review – in light of garlic and onions and morning breath – let's forget this holding your breath thing. You are free to drop your breath.

I'm a little upset that I used a cuss word. My goal was to write an entire book without swearing. I didn't even make it through three full chapters. Some would argue that I could go back and edit that. I could, but that would make me feel like a censor. Censors are the children Curmudgeon Virgins would have had if they ever had sex. Besides, editing takes too much effort. The damn word stands.

I just hope this isn't like a dam bursting. I hope there isn't a proverbial flood of profanity erupting as a result of that one faux pas. Whoa…a proverbial flood of profanity. That is lofty. You'll probably want to incorporate that into your daily conversation as soon as possible. Although I don't think profanity erupts. It just oozes, unless the Supreme Court gets involved. Then it climaxes. I'm also disappointed that I did not mention my good friend Sheryl in this chapter. I will try to do better in the next one.

Chapter IV. – "What We Have Here…" Or: Say What?

I'll bet my dear friend Sheryl would love the following exchange between father and son:

"I know what color God is."

"You do?"

"Yup."

"How did you learn that?"

"When we prayed before eating."

"I…ah…Well – what color is he?"

"He's gray."

"He is?"

"Yes. Today we said, 'God is gray, God is good, let us thank him for our food.'"

Sometimes things are not as we hear them. I'll bet Sheryl would love this one, also:

"I know what God's last name is."

"You do?"

"Uh huh."

"I didn't know there was a last name."

"There is."

"What is it?"

"Zilla."

"God Zilla?"

"Uh huh."

One of those conversations actually happened. In my house. With a relative of mine. The other should have but didn't, so I made it up. I'm not telling which is which. But I love the way communication doesn't happen.

When I was a lad...Wait, I've got to stop laughing before I continue. I don't think I was ever "a lad." A kid maybe. Also a twit, a punk, and a youngster, but a lad? I have no idea where that came from.

So...back in the days of my youth, I used to watch the Mickey Mouse Club. I'm not talking about the modern, Britney Spears, full living color version. I'm talking about the original, black and white, totally corny version. At the end of each episode, as the final song was being sung, the two youngest Mouseketeers sang a duet -- a dorky duet. Their names were Karen and Cubby. That's right, someone actually named a child Cubby – unless it was a nickname – but what five-year-old had a nickname in the 50's? I mean, today the kid could have a nickname, a mullet, a tattoo, and a tongue ring, but not then.

So there was a boy named Cubby, and we all just accepted it and moved on. We never wondered about his last name. Only Annette was allowed to have a last name, but that was after she fled the Mouseketeer Cult and started dancing on the beach with Frankie Avalon. No other Mickey Mousers ever had a last name. In my mind, Cubby's last name was Checker. He was the white, younger brother of Chubby Checker, but Cubby Checker couldn't do the Peppermint Twist so he had to sing a dumb song with Karen somebody every night.

They sang "Now it's time to say goodbye to all our company." It was oh so cute, with deep, meaningful lyrics – the likes of which would not be seen again until disco music appeared. And I couldn't handle the words. Apparently, I ran around my house saying goodbye to all my bumpany – or bump a knee. At least that's the urban legend perpetuated by my parents. And they thought the whole thing was cute. Yuk.

Now I feel obligated to finish the song. "M-I-C-See you real soon. K-E-Y- Why? Because we like you! M-O-U-S-E." I'm tearing up or down.

A person raised on that stuff was in serious danger of living a life full of Shirley Temple re-runs and The Lawrence Welk Show. Fortunately, puberty and the Beatles conveniently coincided to prevent such catastrophe.

I'm not a fan of the, "Back when I was a kid" discourse. I don't like people who constantly talk about, "In my day, things were... whatever they were." But I do understand the temptation. I'm tempted to point out that, back in my day, when I was a kid, we went through puberty with the Beatles, while subsequent generations came of age to Milli Vanilli or The New Kids on the Block or Hannah Montana. I continue to resist the urge to say nah-nah-na-nah-na. I believe my restraint is commendable. I wonder if I left out a "nah."

Apparently, many people misunderstood Credence Clearwater Revival's *Bad Moon Risin'*. After being admonished not to go out tonight, they misunderstood the reason. "There's a bad moon on the rise" became, "There's a bathroom on the right." Not exactly the same message.

I know young kids who, after pledging their allegiance to the flag and the republic for "Richard Stanz," wondered aloud who this Richard Stanz was and what he had done.

For years I thought people were singing, "My body lies over the ocean, my body lies over the sea." I guess I just thought it was a weird song about some outer body experience. When I found out it was my bonnie over there, I wondered, "Bonnie Who? Who is she?"

I'll bet most people reading this chapter have had equal moments of brain and/or hearing malfunction. Many are probably frothing at the bit to share their own stories of incompetence. If that is true, I urge you to:

a) Take the bit out of your mouth – you are not a horse
b) Carefully clean-up the excess froth and learn some self-control, and

c) Send your no doubt hilarious anecdotes to my close, personal friend Sheryl, who will probably write a song about it.

I was tempted to write that Sheryl would have something to crow about, or Crow about, but I'll bet she has heard that so many times she's sick of it. I would never want to make her sick.

So let's just sing – to the tune of the Mickey Mouse theme song. "S-H-E – E is for everyone -- R-Y-L- L because you're lovable -- C-R-O-W." Amen.

Chapter V. – The Expert
Or: When I Grow Up

If and when I grow up – and there is ample evidence that I won't – I hope to be a fired SEC football coach.

I know that might not sound like a lofty goal, but it's my goal just the same.

The SEC stands for the Southeastern Conference – where football is one part activity, two parts religion, and three parts obsession. Why it has six parts is a mystery. Football coaches make more than the U.S. President and the college president combined. Much more.

Currently, Nick "Mr. Warmth" Saban is the highest paid coach in the conference – maybe the world. A great research project would be to find out the salary of each of the twelve college presidents in the SEC and see if their combined salaries are more than Nickie Pooh's annual salary of $4,000,000. It's not a good research project for me, but for someone.

As a result of the competitive nature of this crazy conference and the pressure to win, coaches have extensive contracts. And two of the most beautiful words in the English language were created: buyout clause. That's right, if a coach is going to be fired, he has to be compensated. Royally. Although not with a crown.

These are people being paid millions of dollars not to work. That is my dream job. People whose services are no longer required are given cars, insurance packages, luxury suites, and massive amounts of money. Why are there luxury suites but no luxury sours? And why can't I get one of these jobs?

To be semi-fair to the coaches, theirs is a job with no security. Coaches are hired to be fired, usually by rich boosters who don't know anything. It's like, "We thought you were a genius last year, but this year you took stupid pills. See ya."

Can't beat your arch rival? You're fired. Can't win "the big one?" You're fired. Didn't kiss the correct anatomical parts of the correct boosters? You're fired. Can't take the program to the "next level?" You guessed it -- you're fired. You're fired by people who have no knowledge of the game, or student-athletes, or how to teach. This could be so unfair – but the buyout clause soothes the pain. Only the U.S. President gets a better deal (his, or even hers someday, is for life). Coaches don't get all the secret service, although sometimes they could use it.

Of course, eventually the money coaches get for not working stops coming. After a few years and a few million, the gravy train stops. I wonder why it's called a gravy train. Sounds like something you'd put on your couch potato.

When the gravy train dries up, the fired, disgraced, unfit to coach a little league team, former coaches need a new source of massive revenue. That's when they become experts – also known as T.V. analysts.

The job of the expert is to explain the nuances and intricacies of football to us plebeians. It seems that once a person has been fired, he becomes smarter. If he had been such a great expert earlier, he might not have been fired. Now he is a grid-iron guru, second guessing unfired coaches from the safety of the broadcast booth or television studio. For this service, he makes far more than college professors and presidents, but less than he was making after being fired.

This mentality has caught on in the political arena. Don't you wish it really was an arena? We could lock the politicians in and let them mud wrestle for a while. Instead, we begin this three and a half year process to elect a president. It costs approximately $197,000,000,000,000,000. The election is held in November. From

November until high noon on January 20th, we have a president and a president-elect. Then, at high noon, or low noon if the wrong person got elected, the president-elect becomes president and the old president becomes a has-been with a book deal and plans for a library. Both political parties take a break from bashing each other for almost two full weeks, but after Groundhog Day, it starts again.

At every step of the way, there is an expert telling us what is going on. In this case, expert is a fancy term for guesser. They don't know. But they guess well. No one ever remembers their track record, with the possible exception of me. I remember them guaranteeing that Bill Clinton and George W. Bush would be one term Presidents, that George H.W. Bush would be re-elected, that Howard Dean would win the Democratic nomination, and that Al Gore would be elected President. (Okay, they might have been technically correct on that last one, but...)

Those are just the ones I seem to remember. Imagine what a serious student willing to do some research might discover. With a track record like that, why do they keep getting paid? And why do we keep listening? And why is it called a track record when we are nowhere near a track?

Maybe it's because politics have become a sporting event – a full contact spectator sport. And if you get voted out of office, if you run a campaign that doesn't win, you're like a fired coach without a buyout clause. CNN or MSNBC or Fox News (which is an oxymoron) will be calling. I'll bet these talking heads make more than college professors. I love the phrase "talking heads."

I also like channel surfing, both the phrase and the activity. It is yet another indication of how active a couch carrot can be. "Look at me, I'm not passively watching mindless television, I'm channel surfing." The other day I was hanging ten on my remote control when I came across a new competition – at least it was new to me. It was a memory contest – an actual game to determine who was the best memorizer. I stopped just in time to see the eventual winner demonstrate that he had memorized all fifty-two cards in a well-shuffled deck. Not exactly the NCAA basketball championship game, but still an impressive feat.

I. – Hair Raising Adventure
Or: Mullet Hunting

ve to make fun of people with mullets. I must
humor, but it does make me curious.

, scraggly hair (at least in the back) earn the title
rew the first one? Why? Was it always called a

of mindless amusement influenced by television,
d televangelism, I've decided to make up my own
As an aside, I hope no one was offended by my
ther "tele" types. I could have included telegraph,
eletubbies, but it seemed like over-kill (not to be
der-kill).

llet heads were females. It seems that ancient
sses favored the fashion statement. There is
Cleopatra tried the style, and that Marc Antony
competed to see who could grow one – but since
arly challenged, they failed. However, many toga-
xuals favored the look, and it soon became a staple
es, although not a literal staple, just a figurative
believe that the mullet contributed to the fall of
re and the rise of the Staples™ chain.

didn't rear its ugly head (ha-ha) again until the
n – although it was still not called a mullet - or

I was ready to continu
actually doing a play-by-p
commentator, an analyst, a
the strategy used in this p
that I am easily amused an
I wondered what qualified
he been fired from?

I realize I ended that las
the Curmudgeon Virgins n
would be the most action t
an analyst for a memory co
health care worker. I also wo
ever forgets where his car k

In America, we can tur
now carries the spelling bee
is televised on the Entertair
Why?

We've got extreme spor
biggest competitions appears
The play-by-play announcer
The appropriate oohs and aa
the significance of the six. So
the Travel Channel shows po

That's right, our Travel
Hawaii, Paris, London, and
table though, this one is in Po
you any of the countryside,
the nine of hearts! Two more
a flush, which is what I want
he's working on a straight fl
orientation should matter at

Chapter

My teen-agers
confess, I see th

How did lor
"mullet?" Who
mullet?

In the spirit
telemarketing,
mullet history.
omission of the
telephone, and
confused with

The first m
Egyptian prin
speculation tha
and Julius Caes
they were follic
wearing metro
at the toga-pa
one. Historian
the Roman Em

The mulle
French Revolu

le mullet pu if you speak French. It was known only as long, ugly hair back then. I believe it is the reason the guillotine was invented; although, I can't substantiate that, mainly because I'm too busy writing this book to be distracted by research.

Thanks to the guillotine, the mullet died out – and would have stayed died out if it weren't for Woodstock. All the pictures of long-haired hippies – not to be confused with crew-cut hippies – inspired a young man name Delbert Fussbucket to try to grow his hair in a similar style. What resulted was weird, shaggy, ugly, long hair in the back, but nothing of substance on the top or sides. Delbert was disgusted and was about to give up, but five of his friends loved it and grew matching hair-dos (and a few hair-don'ts). They later donned long, white robes and hung out in airports, but not before others at the high school copied the style.

The school administrators were furious and enacted strict dress codes in an attempt to address the most pressing problem in their school. In fact, they decided that ugly hair was far more disruptive than drugs or violence or poor study habits.

The kids were upset because ugly hair had become their birthright, and they rallied to express their individuality by following the latest fashion. People were suspended and law suits were filed, and by the time they were resolved, the students all had short, gray hair or no hair at all. But the hard feelings remained, and none of this would have been significant except for where it happened. This major hair showdown occurred in Mullet, Nebraska. The mullet is named for a place, not a person.

Recently, the actual transcripts of the trial were released. I have included a brief exchange between the judge and the school principal.

Judge: Are there drug problems in your school?
Principal: Yes.
Judge: Are there problems with teen-age pregnancies?
Principal: Oh yes, indeed.
Judge: Are there fights and other acts of violence?
Principal: Yes.
Judge: Are your SAT and ACT scores where you want them?
Principal: Well...No – Not exactly.

Judge: How is the drop-out rate?

Principal: Um...a...We are trying to improve it.

Judge: So don't you think there are more important problems than ugly hair?

Principal: No ma'am -- I think mulletness is at the root of all evil.

There are people who swear that the judge used the word "idiot" at that point, but it cannot be found in the transcript. Her honor, who dyed her hair, ruled that the school had a right to create its own dress code, no matter how arbitrary and asinine it might be, and so the very fabric of life in Mullet was saved from the subversive hair growers. The principal repeated his long-held belief that growing a mullet was the first step on the road to becoming a terrorist.

Several concerned citizens expressed their concern that Mullet might become a tourist attraction after all the publicity, and several other concerned citizens expressed fear that living in a town that shared its name with an evil hair style was almost like being a Communist, and before the unconcerned citizens knew what was happening, a referendum was passed that changed the town's name to Prudent.

There are no mullets in Prudent, Nebraska, but there are in many other places. My teen-agers go mullet hunting, although not with guns. There are websites and games and contests. There are rules – and an official mullet season. Mullet poaching, or hunting out of season, is considered gauche. There are mullet categories, and a complex point system for spotting the various styles. The military mullet – a crew cut plus a mullet, worn by someone wearing camo, is a valued sighting, second only to the Mohawk mullet.

Malls and airports are excellent hunting grounds, as are NASCAR races and county fairs. So for all you people who think teen-agers are lazy, video game playing wieners, I say, "Shame on you." Mullet hunting is hard work, and serious competition. It encourages travel, enhances physical conditioning, and improves the power of observation.

I'm thinking of starting a mullet hunting fantasy league today. Or maybe tomorrow, I'm a little tired after teaching this history lesson.

Chapter VII. – TV Time
Or: We'll Be Right Back

It was the first football Saturday of the season. I was in My Chair watching *ESPN GameDay*. The crown prince (or is it clown prince?) of the broadcast is Lee Corso. Lee is one of the fired experts discussed previously, perhaps in chapter four.

Wait...hold that thought...I am going to do something totally out of character. I am going to find out exactly what chapter dealt with fired experts...

Upon further review, it was chapter five. I was very close. Writing and research are incredibly stressful and time consuming.

So there I was, getting mentally prepared for the football season, and *GameDay* was going to commercials, plural, even though it is always used as a singular, and Expert Corso said, "Don't touch that dial – we'll be back with our picks – blah, blah, blah, whatever."

Since I was told not to touch my dial, I obeyed. I grabbed the remote and did some channel surfing instead.

The main reason I didn't touch my dial was because my TV was not made in the 50's. I don't have a dial to touch, even if I wanted to. Besides, that would involve getting out of My Chair, walking all the way to the television, and physically moving something attached to the set. Are you kidding me?

I actually remember, vaguely, doing just that. It was hell. Kids today have no idea the hardships we endured back in our day. Fortunately, we are no longer subjected to such trauma and America is a better country because of that.

I wonder how much time has passed since I had a dial. I believe it has been 3.1417 decades – or is that pi? You remember pi. It's that totally useless math thing that has never been used but causes orgasmic excitement in math teachers across America. And it's spelled wrong.

I did return to ESPN in time to see Lee Corso and his much younger, more virile sidekick, Kirk Herbstreit, make their predictions. I have no idea how Herbstreit got this gig – to the best of my knowledge no one has ever fired him. Maybe he's eye candy for the female football fans – also known as the FFF – or F cubed.

Anyway, these two experts make their predictions and we all listen intently, and the games begin, and by halftime of the first game nobody remembers any of the predictions, because Americans have the attention span of a gnat, so no one remembers how many mistakes they made, and thus they are qualified to repeat the process the following week.

One week I wrote down their predictions, along with my own, and I think I did as well as they did, but I lost the paper, which is just as well because it was too difficult to keep track, what with all the coaching and yelling and eating and guzzling going on. I think I stink at the prognostication business – but what do you expect? I've never been fired. I do like the term prognostication business – it sounds like a good retirement job.

The *GameDay* crew gets to spend an entire week studying football games before they make their picks. And I know they make more than rescue workers. It's the American way. Save a life – make a little money. Pick who might win a football game – make a fortune – even if you suck at it – even if you say dorky, outdated things like, "Don't touch that dial."

After the game, Corso went home and listened to oldies on his eight-track while drinking some Ovaltine™. The next morning he shaved with BurmaShave™, threw on some High Karate, grabbed a little dab 'a Brillcream™ for his hair, and had some Quaker Oats™ for breakfast. Then, he began to study the upcoming game, occasionally popping candy from his Pez™ dispenser.

There are eleven teachers in the English department where I teach. I'll bet Corso makes more than all of us combined. That's my education paying dividends. I'm not bitter. And next week, at 10 a.m., I'll watch *College Football GameDay* with my remote in hand from the sanctuary of My Chair, and I'll wonder about my lack of logic – but only for a moment. Let the games begin.

Chapter VIII. – Retirement
Or: Shut Up

I am 56 years old. By the time this gets published, I'll be 57, or 80, I don't know. But right not, I'm 56, and I've taught for over 30 years, so that means everyone, and I do mean every freakin' one, feels compelled to ask me, "When are you going to retire?" That question pisses me off. I don't know why it does – but it does.

It doesn't always piss me off, just 89% of the time. I have some close friends who are just being interested. That's cool. A few have actually retired themselves. It's a friendship thing – a curiosity thing – a normal, conversational thing.

But everyone else who asks – well, I've already expressed my pissed offedness.

It's almost like asking, "Hey, you old fart – are you still teaching?" I want to say, "Yeah, you old dickweed, are you still breathing?"

My eye doctor asks me once a year. My dentist asks me twice a year. I have been introduced to imperfect strangers who:

a) find out I'm a teacher
b) tell me how they hated English
c) ask how long I've been teaching, and
d) immediately ask, "When are you going to retire?"

I want to say, "I don't know – when are you going to get a personality?"

Administrators ask. I want to say, "When you administrate better than I teach, I'll know it's time to quit." I don't. I just shrug. Administrators will be the last to know.

Colleagues ask. Colleagues I've never spent any time with, not counting horrendously long faculty meetings (which is why administrators will be the last to know). "When are you going to quit teaching?"

"I'm not sure – when are you going to start?"

"When ya gonna retire?"

"When I can take Lee Corso's place."

Kids ask. If it's a student who does poorly and is hoping I'll tell him, "Tomorrow," I say, "Not until after you graduate."

It's almost like an accusation. You qualify for retirement – so why are you still here?

I don't feel old. My wife will tell you that I certainly don't act old (she seems to think 12 is my mental age). I've been told that I don't look old. But the minute my age or experience is mentioned, the retirement questions start.

"I will not go gentle into that good night." I know – Dylan Thomas was talking about death and I'm talking about retirement, but the principle is the same. I feel like I'm being charged with the crime of old age. I plead not guilty.

There are people in this country, maybe even a majority of people in this country, who, for reasons that are totally unfathomable, will actually vote for John McCain. John McCain is 16 years older than I am. Many will deem him fit to run the country, but then will wonder if I will continue to run my classroom. Amazing.

It's almost enough to make me root for him. Okay, that's a lie, but ageism isn't nice. Besides, I couldn't vote for him because my dear, sweet, kind friend Sheryl – remember Sheryl? This book is inspired by her. Sheryl would never forgive me if I voted for Diddly Squat.

That's another crazy thing about the writing business. I am writing this sentence on September 5, 2008. I have no idea who will be elected president. By the time I'm done, and the book has been edited and all that other boring, technical stuff, I will know who the president-elect is. Some of my students will also know.

It would be entirely possible (as opposed to partially possible) to go back and edit the political references so they coincide with the political reality. It is my firm hope and belief that by now, having bonded with each other through these pages, you know me better than that. I'm trying to be progressive – always looking forward – driving ahead without a rearview mirror.

It is possible that driving ahead without a rearview mirror is stupid and dangerous and a terrible analogy. I can live with that. It is also possible that the notion of bonding with each other through these pages is:
a)   pathetic
b)   disgusting in a kinky sort of way
c)   cornier than *Hee-Haw*, or
d)   the perfect way to begin my campaign for president.

I didn't mention that I was considering running for president? There is a reason for that. I hadn't thought about it until I sat here – racking my brain – trying to come up with option "d" in the above multiple choice.

I wasn't really racking my brain. Every time I hear that phrase I think of a pool table, and some guy taking a big, white triangle and organizing the cerebellum and the cerebrum and some sort of cortex and all those other medical terms while some other guy waits, chalking his pool stick, waiting to break the tightly racked brain parts. Now you know why our politicians are so scatterbrained. They need to stop racking their brains.

And if I'm president, you will never catch me racking anything.

I'm not saying I'm going to run, I'm just saying I'm thinking about it. Right now, I'm thinking, "Why is it called 'running for president' when nobody actually runs?" Hell, you don't even see a fast walk, although I think it would make for a far more interesting campaign if the candidates were required to actually run. Then it really would be a race. I can think of numerous candidates, in both parties, who I would gladly watch. I'd sit in My Chair and wait for a political race running expert to give his or her analysis of the stride and the strategy. I'd like to suggest Bob Dole and Michael Dukakis.

I think this presidential thing has potential. Eventually, I will retire, and I might need something to do. After thirty years of teenagers, the White House might be a pleasant chance of pace. Or a good retirement home. I wonder if Sheryl would be my running mate. We'd soak up some votes.

Chapter IX. – Working Out Or: Why Bother?

Joan Rivers once said, "I hate housework. You do it once, six months later you have to start all over again." That's how I feel about exercise – working out – getting in shape – whatever you call it.

Remember when Joan Rivers was actually funny? I think I do, although it may be an urban legend. I'm pretty sure it was back in the day when her skin fit. Now it's too tight, and I think that affects humor.

Ms. Rivers is one of those so-called comedians who can only get laughs at the expense of others. It gets old. (Too bad things never get young). Kathy Griffin is the same way. How much talent does it take to trash someone? Especially people who have major problems, are going through rehab, are making a mess of their lives. Let's pile on – kick 'em while they're down – get a cheap laugh at their expense because it makes us feel better about ourselves.

I try not to resort to cheap laughs to feel good about myself. I mean, I do resort to cheap laughs, but it doesn't make me feel good about myself. Even expensive laughs don't work.

That's why I work out, even when I do it inside. Sometimes I'm inside, working out, and I just start feeling so good about myself, because I know that many Americans are not working out, and are therefore inferior to those of us striving for physical perfection.

When they die, they won't feel as good about their lives as I will when I die (probably on a treadmill).

I have pathetic workout habits. I can go for weeks at a time, getting fit and losing weight and feeling healthy, and then something happens, an excuse arises, and I'm done until the next twinge of guilt forces me to try again.

I will blimp up and look like a pregnant man, then I will lose some weight and figure, "Close enough." It's a sad roller coaster ride.

Usually, I don't feel better after working out – just tired. And sore. But it's good for me – so I do it, hoping to get 12-pack abs and buns of titanium, or something like that. Because a 56- year-old man with gray hair and a gut is considered a geezer, whereas a 56-year-old man with gray hair and no gut is considered a thinner geezer. That is something to strive for. Or something for which to strive if ending a sentence with a preposition offends some latent Curmudgeon Virgin gene lying deep within you.

Not that I feel like a geezer in either scenario. I am talking about the perception of others – a perceived societal geezerness, or PSG. PSG is the male equivalent of PMS, only there are no drugs to alleviate the problem, with the possible exception of alcohol.

Sometimes, while using my cross-trainer (who thought up that name?) or rapidly walking a hiking trail, or attempting to play some basketball, I have my loftiest thoughts. It's like a mental adrenaline rush; as if some hyped-up endorphin cruises to my brain and… voila…deep thoughts emerge such as why are lofty thoughts and deep thoughts synonyms when they sound like opposites?

I like lofty thoughts, but sometimes I'm afraid of heights. And I like deep thoughts (unless I get in over my head), but most of all I just like new thoughts. You know the kind, the ones that surprise you – that make you say, "Whoa – that's amazing. Why didn't I already know that?"

I'll bet the real deep thinkers had lots of those experiences. Can you imagine how many times Thomas Edison had those moments? What about Einstein – he probably had migraines from all his epiphanies. I'm happy for an occasional head rush, like the one I got when I first realized the role of the Curmudgeon Virgins in our society, or how Mall Walkers are our best hope for the future, or that John McCain is really Diddly Squat and my dear, sweet, loyal friend Sheryl is better off without him.

If you're cross-eyed and use a cross trainer, can you see straight? Do you have to wear a cross? Is it too much to bear? If you are dressed on the cross trainer, are you a cross trainer dresser? I need to stop working out.

Chapter V. – The Bumper Sticker Or: Pressure

It is less than two months until the 2008 presidential election and I have a political bumper sticker on my vehicle. I'm not trying to write a political book, so I will not mention which candidate the bumper sticker supports, although it clearly is not Diddly Squat.

For most of my life I avoided putting anything on my vehicles, political or otherwise -- I wasn't a bumper sticker sort of guy. It has nothing to do with the fact that the abbreviation for bumper sticker would be...drum roll... I'll bet you don't need me to spell is out for you. BS, BS, BS. Just because someone doesn't need it spelled out doesn't stop others from spelling it out. It's what makes us Americans.

I am not a recent convert to the BS wisdom. I've always enjoyed a good BS, from afar, but I never personally indulged. My bumpers were pristine, virginal territory. They lost their virginity to a UT sticker and a *Jimmy Buffett for President* sticker (subheading: *Put a Real Pirate in the White House*).

Then I got a new truck, and for three years, it was stickerless. Last week that changed, and I've felt considerable pressure ever since.

Let's pretend (isn't this fun?) that you support candidate X. You may or may not have an X BS, but you support X. You're driving along, minding your own business, and actually paying attention to the important task of trying to arrive safely to your destination. You are not talking on a cell phone or putting on make-up or eating a seven course meal. You are simply cautiously driving. Suddenly you are cut-off by a Hummer, forcing you to swerve or jam on the brakes to avoid a massive collision. Just as the adrenaline and the cuss words begin to flow, you notice candidate Y's bumper sticker on the back of the Hummer.

Immediately, you think:
a) What do you expect from a Y supporter?
b) Y supporters can't drive or think, or
c) Y supporters are dangerous scum, or
d) All the expletives deleted from the Nixon tapes.

Actually, you think all those thoughts in that order, which would be a terrible generalization except that all is fair in love and politics.

There is no attempt here to paint Y supporters as gas guzzling Hummer drivers. The same thought would apply if the Y supporter drove a hybrid (ha-ha – that's a good one) or a vintage Pinto.

I don't believe I've ever actually seen a vintage Pinto. I know I've never written those words together until now. I also know that the abbreviation for vintage Pinto is VP – and I can think of numerous comparisons between our recent vice-presidents and Pintos, but that would be too easy.

But now, as an X supporter, I feel the added pressure of not giving Y supporters reason to cast aspersions on X supporters. I've never actually cast an aspersion. I don't know if you use a fishing pole or just throw them like a net. But I worry about aspersions being thrown my way. I am carrying the weight of the X campaign on my driving abilities. It is not easy.

And I put the bumper sticker on my window. It's not even a true bumper sticker. I hope that doesn't hurt my candidate's chances.

I wonder how many votes are won for someone because of bumper stickers or lawn signs. Clearly they work; otherwise both parties would not use them. How much money is spent on them?

TV ads are worse. They work. People make up their minds based on commercials. We know that from the gazillion dollars a second people pay for Super Bowl ads.

And then there is the internet. Start an internet rumor and sway the masses. Candidate X wants your guns. He also wants to give your five-year-old condoms and make abortion mandatory.

Candidate Y, on the other hand, has had twelve affairs, two illegitimate children, wants to invade twelve countries, and will bring back the draft. Yea – Rah-Rah -- Internet.

I wonder if we are the most gullible country on the plant. I'll bet twelve-year-olds could, in about 15 minutes, devise a better system for electing a president. I seem to be using the number 12 frequently. I should change that.

In August of 2008, the two candidates raised a combined total of $114,000,000. That is one month of fund-raising. Think of all the bumper stickers and yard signs and TV ads that will buy. What a great use of money, far better than spending it on schools or the environment or roads or Mall Walker protection programs.

Every person I know says they are sick of the constant commercials. Every democrat and republican friend I have says the campaigns are too long. I have never met a single person who wants to see more time and money spent on this process. That is why I am starting my campaign for the 2016 presidential election today.

Actually, I think there are several others, in both parties, who have already started. Maybe I'll wait to see how this race turns out. And while I am waiting, you can rest assured that I will be driving carefully, trying to set a good example for all BSXers to follow. Or you can rest unassured if you are a BSYer. We can still be friends – after the election.

Chapter XI. – The End of an Era
Or: My Fellow Americans

This is a book. This is only a book. But if it were a TV show, or a movie, the following, poignant scene would play out as you valiantly fought to hold back your tears. You would fail, because holding back tears is impossible – no matter how hard you try to push them back from wherever they came.

The camera would focus on a podium. A gray-haired 56-year-old geezer, this month with only a tiny gut, would stride to the podium. That would be me. I would look at the people in the audience, both of them, and I would say, "Lady and gentleman, after careful consideration, I have decided not to seek the office of President of the United States."

I would then wince – not from physical pain, but from the realization that I just uttered an incredible stupid, clichéd statement. I might feel compelled to help all who might, "Seek the office of President of the United States." I'd tell them, "It's that oval thing in the big, white mansion at 1600 Pennsylvania Avenue. Seek no more"

Seek the office – indeed. Like we're playing hide-and-seek. "Where's the office?"

"I don't know."

"What are you going to do?"

"I'm going to seek it."

"Who hid it?"

"I'm not sure – I'm guessing Dick Cheney."

"Well…Good luck – I hope you find it."

I'd start to apologize for my initial statement and simply announce that I am not running or, since you now know about my poor exercise habits, walking for president.

If someone were to ask why I was no longer a candidate, I would tell them that being president is a stupid job, and I already have a stupid job, remember? I teach. And I didn't have to campaign for it.

Some…okay one of my supporters might beg to differ. I would say, "Cindy, (that's my wife's name) you don't have to beg. Just differ."

She'd point out the $400,000 presidential salary, the nice house, the limo, the helicopter, Air Force One, and the fact that Sheryl would gladly perform at our house.

I'd say, "Dumplin'…" I always call her dumplin' at moments like this. Apparently there has never been a moment like this before. "Dumplin'" just came out of the purple. But I may use it from now on. Then I'd explain in my usual, calm, rational manner why being president is a stupid job and she'd be swayed (and perhaps a little awed) by my logic, and we'd remain in East Tennessee.

Here's just one example of why the Presidency is not for me. It's a Saturday. A beautiful fall Saturday – maybe even the third Saturday in October. For those not obsessed with SEC football, that means Tennessee is about to play Alabama. The game is at Neyland Stadium. The *GameDay* crew is there. Lee Corso is about to put on the headgear of his pick to win this titanic battle, then the ship hits an iceberg and…no wait -- wrong scenario…Corso reaches for the headgear and BOOM. The mood is broken. The phone rings or some presidential lackey interrupts with some so-called crisis requiring immediate presidential attention. Something like a natural disaster, or a man-made disaster, a financial crisis, or a war. Maybe those pesky Russians invaded Georgia again. And I miss Corso's selection. All in the name of trying to run a country. Ridiculous.

When most SEC fans heard that Russia invaded Georgia, they thought of the state – and the football team in Athens – and UGA the mascot – and they were ready to help the Russians. Then they discovered it was a foreign country and lost interest. As President, one is not supposed to lose interest, although one could argue that some have.

So now I'm a POP – a pissed-off President – and after threatening people with the Marines, I'd calm down and promise to look into the crisis during halftime. And even if My Chair were moved to the White House, it wouldn't be the same. How much guzzling could I do, knowing I had some crisis to attend to? Although it appears some presidents have done some serious guzzling in the past. And how could I concentrate on coaching and all those other important activities?

Nope – I'm not about to miss my football Saturdays, even Lee Corso and the headgear. I wish I had a headgear. I'd shift into over-drive and…I don't like where this is going. Forget that.

And that's only one of the reasons being president is a stupid job. There's also:
1) Trying to work with those dorks in the other party
2) Answering questions from those dorks in the media
3) Having to appear interested when people tell you their problems
4) Kissing ugly, crying babies
5) Having to act all polite and presidential in public – even at sporting events, and
6) Beginning the re-election campaign one hour after the inaugural address.

And if all of that isn't enough, there is a dirty little word that makes even considering the job a stupid career choice. That word is vetting. I would have to be vetted, which sounds like something you'd do to your Golden Retriever, but actually means scrutinized beyond the bounds of a proctologist. Some people, apparently called vetters, would push and pry and investigate each and every word and thought and action since childbirth. Every friend, relative, acquaintance, enemy, colleague, or local wino would also be vetted.

It's not that I'm afraid of what they'd find. I have no skeletons in my closet. If I did, my wife would say, "Get that damn skeleton out of the closet." I don't think that "damn" should be held against me because I was only quoting my wife. Cindy cusses like...well... she almost never cusses, except when she's around skeletons, but I was not going to say she cusses like a sailor, because that's silly. Why sailors? Or drunken sailors for that matter? Who decided to single them out for cussing immortality?

I'll bet prisoners cuss more. Why don't we say someone cusses like a prisoner? In fact, if you say that, people will look at you like you're dumb, even when you are making the most sense.

But if I had to pick on a group for cussing, I'd pick the most foul-mouthed group in America. I'd say, "My wife was cussing like a president." And I'm not just talking Richard Nixon here. How many bad words were exchanged between Bill and Hillary when the whole Lewinski thing...well I was going to say when the Lewinski thing heated up, but that would be a terrible choice of words. But you get the idea.

I'll bet "W" is in the top five presidential cussers. Popularity at forty percent? Thirty? Twenty? You know he used pre-emptive swearing. I'll bet he called the old vintage Pinto into the office for some commiseration cussing, except for when Dick shot that guy. I'll bet there was some different cussing that day.

But presidents rarely cuss in public. Not dignified. And from now on, whenever I need a cliché to indicate how badly someone is cussing, I'm sticking with, "He cusses like a drunken president," even though I won't be a president. Which is sad, because of Air Force One and Sheryl's performance. And sad for the country, because I can pronounce nuclear. Oh well – America's loss. Unless Sheryl calls and says she'll be my vintage Pinto. In that case, I'm coming out of retirement.

Chapter XII. – Dickweeds Among Us
Or: Look Out

I have walked through the valley of the dickweed – and it is not pretty. America is being overrun with dickweeds, and I say, "Enough is enough." As opposed to, "Enough is not enough."

The next sentence, this one, was supposed to contain a definition of the word dickweed, along with an explanation for why the word is written as one word instead of two. I even decided to break with tradition and actually look up the word – you know, in one of those old-fashioned dictionary things. Imagine my chagrin when I discovered that dickweed was not in my dictionary.

I found dickcissel – a sparrow-like bird found in central North American – but no dickweed. I attributed that to the fact that my personal dictionary was printed during the Johnson administration, so I found a newer, Bush-era dictionary. Same results. I was annoyed and exhausted after this lengthy investigation – which served as a vivid reminder of why I gave up research years ago, but I was also determined to give my readers – gentle and ungentle – the definition they deserve.

So I googled. Yes, I did – right there in my living room. I googled, which sounds disgusting, I know. "Did you see that baby? He googled all over his mother's new blouse." But this google produced a motherload of dickweed information. I wonder why there isn't a fatherload of information, especially about a word like dickweed, which sounds masculine to me.

There were all kinds of sites devoted to this word, including an urban dictionary that was truly educational. I selected the definition "(n. pejorative slang) an undesirable person." This may have come from Wiktionary – an offspring of the incredibly stupid Wikipedia. Wikipedia is a place in cyberspace where any fool with a mouse can edit any piece of information ever posted. And the creators of this site didn't anticipate people being mischievous? Really? It's like cyberspace graffiti.

I didn't really discover the history of dickweed, but if you go to Wikipedia or Wiktionary, you might now find, thanks to my efforts, the following origin:

Once upon a time, there was a college co-ed named Mary Alice Puffin. She attended Smith College in the early 50's, where she majored in English literature. She pictured a career of writing romance novels and working for some fashion magazine until her senior year. That's when she fell in love with her sociology professor – Richard Weed. They married, and Mary Alice Puffin did something unheard of during that time period. She dropped her given middle name – Alice – and kept her last name. This was long before former first lady/presidential candidates made it fashionable.

Some believe Mary Alice Puffin didn't like the name Alice – she got tired of all those wonderland allusions. Others maintain it was her initials – M.A.P. that caused the change. Apparently, some crude members of the male persuasion were always saying witty things like, "Hey M.A.P. – show me Hawaii," or, "If you're a M.A.P., where's your inset?" Whatever the cause, Mary Alice Puffin became Mary Puffin Weed. Remember, this was before the 60's, so it was not considered a drug thing then.

Richard and Mary Puffin Weed wed and bred. A son was born. They wanted to call him Richard the Second, but that sounded too British. They didn't like "junior," so they called him Little Richard – but only for a short time. Another Little Richard became a rock icon, and they were concerned about all those *Tutti Frutti* references, so they just called him Dick.

Dick grew up to become the first major C.E.O. to get a multi-million dollar buyout while his company went bankrupt. Dick seemed depressed, and one day he jumped off of a skyscraper. Stunned observers watched Dick hurtle toward the earth, but then an enormous golden parachute opened, and one observed, "There goes that scumbag Dick Weed."

In no time, the two words became synonymous with any and all scumbags, and the two proper nouns became a one word common noun. It seemed inevitable – and if dickweed hadn't evolved, dicknixon or dickcheney would have. We might be uttering phrases like, "That Dick Cheney is a dicknixon" if Dick Weed hadn't come along.

No amount of research can answer how and when and why American became the land of dickweeds, but it did. I have become a dickweed expert while writing this book, and I believe there are three major categories. They are: the innocuous dickweed (or ID), the major dickweed (or MD), and the colossal dickweed (or CD).

The IDs are the most common, but the least bothersome. They're like gnats. If you are waiting at a stop sign to pull out, and a car is approaching from your left, and that car suddenly turns onto the very road you are on, but that car did not use a signaling device, and now you are stuck for who knows how long because of the traffic, you have had a close encounter with an ID. It's not a major trauma, just a mild inconvenience – but a needless one. Those turn signal levers aren't heavy or hard to find.

IDs are always in front of you at the checkout line – appearing shocked at the total of their purchase, fumbling for money or beginning to write a check after the total has been rung up. None of this is life-altering. All of this is the jock-itch of daily existence. Then there are the MDs. If you go to a movie, you will see their presence, and hear their impact.

The last time I went to the theatre, I was politely and frequently reminded to turn off my cell phone. For those capable of reading, words to that effect were shown on the screen. I was reminded before the previews, after the previews, and just before the movie began. For MDs, this is not sufficient.

One MD actually answered his phone and had a conversation while the movie was playing.

If I am watching a UT sporting event at home and the phone rings, (which rarely happens) I don't answer. I know it's an MD calling. If I attend an event in person, I know an MD will be sitting behind me – criticizing every play and coaching decision and providing a non-stop commentary more annoying that Dick Vital on helium.

MDs run for elected office and often win, although not as frequently as CDs. (That's a colossal duckweed -- in case you are an MD with a short attention span).

This past summer, my wife and I visited one of the most uniquely beautiful ecosystems on the planet – Yellowstone National Park. Words fail to capture how much I love that special place. One would think that dickweeds would not be allowed there. One would, in fact, be thinking like a dickweed if one thought that.

While it is true that IDs and MDs were not present, and while it is true that the number of colossal dickweeds was small, it is also true that the few CDs who actually found the park performed extra-ordinary fetes of dickweedness.

News bulletin: There are animals in Yellowstone. Big Animals. Big Wild Animals. Big Wild Dangerous Animals – although none as dangerous as the humans. There are also signs – warnings – pamphlets – and park rangers – all trying to explain how to avoid being trampled or becoming dinner. Most people get this. The CDs do not.

One CD parked next to a sign about staying away from the elk and proceeded to hike directly toward – say it with me – an elk. The elk ran away, so nobody could view him, but he could have easily run at the CD.

Bison are dangerous. They kill more people than grizzlies (one of the few factual statements in this book). They weigh more than Rhode Island, and they are faster than Secretariat. Okay, that's sick, because Secretariat is dead, so he's not too fast. Apparently I have a touch of ID myself. But people will crowd the bison. They will honk at them if they are crossing the road too slowly. And they will place their children with their back to the bison to get a compelling picture of a child in front of a wild beast. Good picture – stupid move.

We saw two cars that might need new transmissions because they got stuck on a mound when they ran off the road while watching elk.

But the king of the CDs, the absolute CD grand pubah was the father and mother who were encouraging their son to throw corn into the river that was the spawning ground of the cut throat trout. They were standing next to a sign that forbid such activity. There are many compelling reasons why what they were doing is biologically stupid. My wife and I were rapidly hiking past them. I saw the sign and the corn feeding. A voice inside me kept saying, "Ignore this. It is a test. It is only a test – a test of the dickweed network. Don't say anything."

I wanted to listen to that voice. I tried, but as we passed this family, clearly doing what the park officials did not want them to do, I found myself saying, "Golly gee, kind sir, would you please read the sign?" That might not be an exact quote. It may have been more of an order – like "Read the sign!" There may have been an adjective thrown in – I'm not sure. We just kept walking, but the man yelled profanities. I'll bet his son was proud.

Now here's the thing. I have no qualms telling my friends about the CD who fed fish next to a sign warning visitors not to feed the fish. My friends all agree that he is, well… he's a colossal dickweed.

But what about his friends? This guy was not pleased with me. You know he went home, and when people asked about his vacation, he said, "It was great, except for this one jerk who told me to read this dumb sign about not feeding the spawning fish. I mean, my son and I were just givin' 'em some corn – ya know? Where's he get off buttin' in?"

And his friends would agree – and cuss words would be said – and Pabst Blue Ribbon guzzled -- and one would say, "Next thing ya know they'll want to take our guns." Heads would nod and blood would boil (although not literally) and I would be the CD of their world.

I can live with that, because I know my sweet, dear, long-time friend Sheryl would be on my side.

This chapter made me tired. There is more to this dickweed stuff than I thought. I may have to revisit this later.

Chapter XIII. – A Serious One
Or: I Really Miss Him

Two weeks from today is Election Day. This long, historic, 2008 campaign is almost over. And something is missing.

Actually, it is not something but someone. Tim Russert is not here to enjoy this, and we are worse for it.

Permanently etched in my mind is Tim with a white board saying, "Florida, Florida, Florida" during the 2000 election. I read his book – his loving tribute to his father. I watched him take the longest running TV show – *Meet the Press* – and make it his own. To steal a line from Dan Fogelberg, he ran his show with, "A thundering velvet hand."

And I watched Tim receive a memorial tribute worthy of any dignitary.

He was that rare man who could be tough and compassionate. He inspired confidence. His zest for life and his intellectual curiosity knew no bounds.

For me, and I suspect millions of others, if Tim Russert said it, it was true. I trusted him – something rarely said about the celebrities who flicker on our TV screens and serve us the latest, temporary "truth." He had depth, substance, integrity, enthusiasm, character, and a personality and sense of humor bigger than his beloved Buffalo.

No one captured the essence of Tim Russert better than Tom Brokaw. He talked about the competitive nature of the news business. He spoke of the competitors who resorted to the latest technological improvements in an attempt to beat him. Then he pointed out that, no matter what the latest style or technology or glitz, nothing has ever been more effective at educating the public than Tim Russert with a whiteboard.

Clearly, there are implications here for educators. Clearly, Tom Brokaw got it right. Then Brokaw did something at the memorial service that truly touched my heart. He reached into a bag and pulled out a mug – and a beer he had taken from Tim's refrigerator. It wasn't just any beer – it was Tim's beer – Rolling Rock™. He spoke lovingly of their relationship and he promised a grieving father that, on election night, he would pour one of Tim's beers and drink a toast to his late colleague, and his father. Tim Russert wouldn't have it any other way.

And I will join Mr. Brokaw. Whether I am celebrating or crying in my beer, it will be Tim's beer – and I will think of him and Big Russ and Tom Brokaw as I hoist my mug and toast the very best of those who tried to make sense of our often nonsensical political process. And I will cry sad yet grateful tears, because I miss Tim Russert.

Chapter XIV. –Long Live Live
Or: Reruns

The other night, *Saturday Night Live* was a rerun. It was still called *Saturday Night Live*, even though it wasn't. I'm not saying it should be called *Saturday Night Dead*, but it should not be called live if it isn't. *Saturday Night Rerun* works for me.

It was like so many shows from the past, "Filmed before a live audience." Big Whoop. (Note – Watch me resist the temptation to mention dead audiences). I want my live shows to be live. I don't think that's asking too much.

Which brings me to the word spelled L-I-V-E. Sometimes it is pronounced differently, as in the sentence, "I live in Tennessee." It violates the vowel-consonant – silent "e" rule, not that rule violation is unusual in our language. Why don't we spell it L-I-V instead? We drop the stupid "e" when we add – "ing" – so why not just drop it all together?

Mark Twain once lamented our country's insistence that there only be one way to spell words. He suggested multiple approaches. Apparently the Curmudgeon Virgins were alive during his time. Twain understood the need for creative thinking and spelling. If he were alive, he might liv in Tennessee. See how much easier that sentence is to read with "proper" spelling? He might even host *Saturday Night Live*.

I like visualizing historical figures in modern settings: Twain on T.V., Cleopatra on the cover of *Cosmopolitan*, Nero at the Grand Ole Opry, Washington on a luxury liner, and Lincoln safely seated at the movies or driving a car – a Lincoln no doubt.

I suppose it could work both ways – modern people back in "olden days." Maybe Paris Hilton could be on the Mayflower, or "W" with Lewis and Clark, or Stephen Colbert searching for the fountain of youth.

Maybe this last idea isn't so good. It is possible that it is one of those situations that seemed so much better in my head than it does on paper. I hate that. I really should edit this out.

I am serious about the L-I-V-E thing. This chapter is titled, "Long Live Live." It would be so much better if it was "Long Liv Live." But if I did that, grammar check would go crazy, and uptight readers would think less of me than they already do, and the prudes who make up the base of a certain political party would view it as yet another example of America's moral decay – thus threatening our credibility as a world power and the very fiber of our society. Writers face far more pressure than the average reader might imagine.

I wonder who the average reader might be. I wonder if you wonder if you – the person reading this sentence – are average. Let me assure you that you are not. Clearly, you are far above average, as indicated by your impeccable taste in reading material. In fact, I am convinced that you are in the top one percent of all the readers in the universe. It's those others who are average – or below average. You, and I, and Sheryl Crow, and certain members of my family, and a few close friends, are trying to rise above the constraints of the Curmudgeon Virgins, and I am honored to be on this quest with you, just as I am proud that I resisted the temptation to mention dead audiences. I think that last sentence is the longest one in the book. I don't care, and I'm sure that you – a top one percent reader, don't either. I will not give up. Long liv America.

Chapter XV. – Diddly Squat Revisited Or: Will this Election Ever End?

I was thinking about this incredible epic I am currently writing when an idea popped into my head. It only hurt a little, probably because it wasn't a very big idea. I am now going to share this with you. Ready?

It is possible that I have confused some people by the way I have used the words diddly squat. Not the top one percent – like you – but those average and below average readers (i.e. – dickweeds). Ha-ha-ha. That was my rapier-like wit attempting humor. Dickweeds don't read books – or signs. I was searching for a group to make fun of, and I didn't want to offend republicans or televangelists or teen-agers, so I went with…well, you know.

My point is that I have used the words diddly squat in two different ways. This is unacceptable – and I am going to rectify that situation. I like the word rectify. It sounds…kinky.

"Say baby – you want to rectify?"

"Not tonight – I have a headache."

I digress. This epic saga began with the song lyrics from my dear, lifelong, closest soul-mate and friend Sheryl Crow. The song bemoaned her lack of digital and diddly squat. I believe I covered that topic fully and, in my humble opinion, beautifully. Somehow, in later chapters, the words diddly squat morphed into a reference to John McCain. I don't remember how or why this happened. I'm too lazy to go back and read it. I'm not sad that it happened – I just don't want people to be confused.

For example, a below average reader might jump (or at least hop) to the conclusion that Sheryl Crow was singing about John McCain. On behalf of my buddy Sheryl, let me say, "No- No- No- a thousand times No." I mean really...Just the idea...The image...I can't finish the thought or the sentence...I'm...I'm trembling at the concept...

So let me rectify, or clarify, or testify. If I am talking about generic, unspecific, run-of-the-mill, average, song lyric diddly squat, it will be written in lower-case letters. If I am referring to the presidential candidate, it was be written in upper-case letters (i.e. – capital letters for the below average reader). Thus, if a certain nominee doesn't have anything, I would write, "Diddly Squat does not have diddly squat." I hope that clarifies the confusion (as opposed to confusing the clarification).

Speaking of Diddly Squat, it is possible that he will be in the oval office when this is published. If that happens, I may be in trouble with:

A) The I.R.S.
B) The F.B.I.
C) The C.I.A.
D) The R.N.C.
E) Hank Williams, Jr.

Then again, he might have a sense of humor about the whole thing (he did pick a moose-hunting hottie as a running mate). By the way, who coined the phrase "running mate?" It is a curious term, since the two people neither run nor mate. Most of us are thankful for that. And who created the idea of "coining a phrase." That's just weird.

Since my decision not to run for president, I have spent time watching this current campaign – although you can't really spend time – at least not like you spend money. I believe that this is the craziest campaign I have ever seen. I know people seem to say that every four years, but I'm serious, and I'm not just crying wolf here. I've only cried wolf one time in my entire life, and that was in Yellowstone where I actually saw one.

For the rest of my life, I may be haunted or permanently scarred by the images of this campaign, expressed here in stream of consciousness.

Inexperience...Too old...Too black...Not black enough... $150,000 in clothing purchases...Joe Sixpack...Joe the plumber... $700,000,000,000 bailout...Wasilla...Muslim... Socialist...The patriotic part of America...Scranton...Flag pins...$150,000,000 raised in one month...Anchorage Barbie...100,000 people at the rally...Out of Touch...Tax and Spender...Out of Ideas...I know how to...The polls...My friends...Out of Time...Change...Bill Ayers... Charles Keating...Stock Market...Acorn...What do you read?... Barracuda...Red State...Swing State... Blue State...Communist... Terrorist...Colin Powell...The First Dude...Undecided...Arab... Elite...Liberal...Media...Iraq...Bomb, Bomb, Bomb...Tax Cuts... Small Business...Golden Parachute...The SEC...Bernanke...al qaeda...Stimulus...Change...My friends...Change...My friends... Change

It makes me tired just listing this partial list of the images. I cannot imagine the fatigue factor of actually campaigning.

One of these guys will have spent two years working toward this job – having every word and action twisted and psychoanalyzed – only to lose. He will have raised and spent millions of dollars, faced unrealistic expectations, uttered hundreds of thousands of words, faced the pressure of three debates with 70,000,000 people watching, and in the end, he will give a classy concession speech and, like an old soldier, simply fade away. He may be the lucky one.

The other guy will do the same things – keep the same crazy schedule – and win. Now he will have to govern. He will have to try to work with the other, pissed-off party. He will select a cabinet – which sounds like something you put dishes in – appoint all kinds of people, have a brief honeymoon, and then begin the slow process of becoming unpopular. Or the fast process – it just depends.

And then it will be time to think about re-election. What a system. It barely leaves time for abusing power, misappropriating money, spying on citizens, paying back enemies, or invading other countries.

I am so glad I am not going to run for president. I'd rather liv in peace and bitch about the current leader instead. It's the American way.

Chapter XVI. – The Boxer
Or: Life in the Past Lane

Once upon a time, back in the 60's or 70's, I saw a cartoon that was…well…cute. Cute is an interesting word if it is said with just the right amount of sarcasm. So is delightful. And adorable. This particular cartoon, the cute one, featured a hippie child saying to his parents, "But I've got to be a non-conformist. How else can I be like all my friends?" If this were an audio book, I would include a rim shot. But the point is valid.

Many of the teen-agers at my school…Whoa – What was that? My school? It isn't my school – I don't own it. It's not even named after me, although after this book is published it might be. Allow me to try again. Many of the teen-agers at the school where I teach listen to a genre of music known as "alternative." Exactly what it is an alternative from is unclear – but it is very popular. In fact, alternative is now mainstream, which is weird. If a person wanted to listen to a real alternative, he or she would listen to opera.

People who sing opera have the best voices in the world. No contest. Do I listen to opera? Never. Why? Because I can't be bothered with great voices telling poignant stories. I listen to classic rock and roll.

If one athlete is far inferior to another, it is said that he can't even carry the superior guy's jock strap. I don't know why that is said, but it is. I don't know if the inferior athlete actually wants to carry the superior athlete's jock strap – in fact, I hope he doesn't. But use that phrase around any group of athletic supporting people, and they know what is being said.

I think there should be jock strap equivalents in other areas. Like music for example. If one singer or type of singer is clearly inferior to another, what would people say? "Hey, that guy can't even carry his pitch pipe?" No – that's not it. Can't carry his tune in a bucket? Nope. Can't carry his mic stand? Warmer. I'll bet Sheryl would know.

Same for politics. The inferior equivalent (hereafter the I.E.) might be, "He can't even carry her stump speech."

I admit, that's pretty weak also. But the concept of the I.E. has potential, and that is why I am challenging you – the top one percent, to identify an area and create your own I.E.s. It's a creative exercise. Maybe it will become a contest. Send your ideas to my B.F.F. Sheryl. I'd run it myself, but I'm very busy with another project.

But whatever you do, do <u>not</u> think outside the box. If you do, you will be like the non-conformist trying to be like his friends. You will become mainstream alternative. In short (or in long) you will become a cliché, or an oxymoron, or both.

The first person to suggest that people should think outside the box was probably being creative. The box may have represented thinking that is confined – "boxed in" – unoriginal. So one person finds an original way to express a thought and the rest of the world, instead of finding their own original expression, copies that one. As a result, every club, organization, T.V. show, football coach, politician, and motivational speaker now exhorts all of us to think outside the box.

That is why I have decided to be original – unique – different. I am going to do all of my thinking smack dab in the middle of the box (assuming I can find one that is big enough). It may be lonely in there, but that's the price one pays for bucking the outside the box trend.

Right this moment, as I sit in my box, writing this sentence, I've had several inside the box thoughts. For example, I'm wondering why I used the words "smack dab" in the previous paragraph. Smack dab? What dah hell is that? And why are they a pair? I wouldn't say "Smack in the middle of the box," nor would I say, "Dab in the middle..." But I did say smack dab in the middle...It is difficult to express my chagrin, so I will ignore that and move on.

My next inside the box thought was about motivational speakers. How does one get to be a motivational speaker? Is it genetic? What happens if a motivational speaker doesn't feel like going to work? Is there a toll free hotline he or she can call? How come some of them are so boring?

And my final thought from the box (because it's getting stuffy in here) is this. I would rather listen to Bob Dylan than Luciano Pavarotti, even though, musically speaking, Dylan can't carry Pavarotti's jock strap – and not just because of the size. And I'm okay with that as I listen to my iPod™ in the comfort of my box.

Chapter XVII. – Dickweeds Revisited Or: We Know Who You Are

I am aware that I have already written about dickweeds. I have tried to address the history and the degree to which dickweeds impact our society. But the subject is too large for a single chapter, so I'm writing another one. If people would just stop being dickweeds, I'd gladly stop writing about it. I'd say the chances of that happening are about the same as the Chicago Cubs winning the World Series five years in a row. By the way, how presumptuous is it to call it the World Series when most of the world doesn't get to compete? Not that the Cubs care.

Remember Jeff Foxworthy's, "you might be a redneck if..." routine. I'm tempted to just substitute dickweed for redneck, but I think being a copy cat is a form of dickweedness, so I'll just list my most recent encounters or observations. Dickweeds:

A) Call meetings late on Friday afternoons. I believe that 68.3 percent of all bosses are dickweeds.
B) Enjoy telemarketing.
C) Build themselves up by tearing others down.
D) Celebrate scoring a touchdown by acting like a third grader.
E) Steal political signs from people's yards. Apparently, there are democratic, republican, and independent dickweeds. Shame on all of you.

F) Fail to keep promises and appointments – especially those who stand you up after you have taken time off from work to meet them at your house.

G) Take crying babies to fancy restaurants where you are celebrating an important milestone – like a new Sam Adams beer or a reunion tour of your favorite 70-year-old rock band.

H) Make their lack of intelligence a virtue while ridiculing someone who is smart. This is especially true in political contests.

I) Swear they will move out of the country if their candidate doesn't win. That's not what makes them a dickweed. What makes them a dickweed is:

    1) Their candidate does not win

    2) After getting our hopes up, they don't move.

J) Are Toppers.

It is possible that some may not be familiar with the term "Topper." I will explain.

A topper is a person who always, as in every single time, has a story or experience that is far superior to any that you have.

For example, if you went to work and complained about it being two degrees below zero at your house, rest assured it was ten below at Topper's. If you went fishing and caught a whale, Topper went fishing and caught six whales, all bigger than yours. (I'm not talking a literal whale here – just a figurative one). No matter what the topic or situation, Topper has been there and done that – and he or she has done it more often or better than you ever dreamed of doing it.

Typically, Toppers have two basic introductory sentences that let you know you are about to be topped. Of course, there are myriad variations on these two. The first is, "That's like the time when..." That intro. is followed by a lengthy monologue that may not be anything at all like your situation, but that doesn't matter. When the monologue is done, you will have been topped.

The second, less subtle intro. is the simple, "That's nothing. This one time…" Then the pattern continues – lengthy monologue ending with you being topped.

Every place I have worked has had a Topper. It's like a law, or a commandment – Thou shalt work with at least one Topper. It does make life interesting. I worked with one Topper who was so bad that we had contests to see who could top the Topper. We'd create scenarios where he couldn't go last. We'd invent things (some would call them lies, but I prefer justifiable truth stretches) and create elaborate strategies just to beat this obnoxious dickweed at his own game. I'm not suggesting this was mature, or a productive use of work time, or an appropriate educational practice. I am suggesting it was fun and one hell of a morale booster.

There is a close cousin to the Topper genre of dickweed. It is the Verbal Diarrhea king or queen. This is another form of V.D. This person doesn't try to top you; he or she doesn't have to. This individual just starts talking and doesn't stop until it is time to leave. Your neck hurts from nodding your head, which you do to make it appear that you are still listening. Of course, you're not, you quit after the first sentence, not that this clueless creep knows or cares. He or she just keeps on talking, like a politician on speed. I'll bet every workforce has at least one such person.

I find that writing about dickweeds is a grueling, energy-sapping, headache producing activity. It is also good therapy. I would like to thank you for participating in that therapy. I feel so much closer to all of you.

Chapter XVIII. – Election Eve
Or: Long Live the Kinks

Twas the night before election
And all through the land
People were hoping
It would turn out as planned

The Democrats were nestled
All smug in their beds
And Republicans were hopeful
Of an upset instead

Enough. Yet another Samuel Clement Moore rip-off. The poor guy. I was just trying to kill time. Not literally. Killing time sounds... criminal. Disclaimer: No time was hurt or killed in the writing of this book.

I hate waiting. Patience is not my strong suit. I actually have a nice, black pin-stripe, but that's a different subject. I'm talking about my lack of patience – my weak suit.

Remember the rock group The Kinks? If you answered no you have no idea what you are missing. For the rest of you, sing with me: *"So tired/ Tired of waiting/ Tired of waiting for you."* The word "you" has about twelve syllables – it doesn't sound the same if you just read it.

I'm tired – so tired of waiting. I spend my life waiting – waiting for the light to change – for the game to start – for the commercial to end. I continually find myself saying, "I can't wait for...something." Fill in the blank with the next BIG THING. I can't wait for Christmas, for spring break, for football season, for basketball season, for summer. I can't wait for my kids to visit, to go on a vacation with my wife, for the next book or CD from my favorite author or singer. Of course, saying, "I can't wait" is stupid. Clearly I can wait – I have waited successfully each and every time I said I could not. But I don't want to wait – I hate to wait. I want what I want and I want it now. I believe that makes me a five-year-old.

It also seems that I am wishing my life away. That is a terrible thing to do. A person needs to live in the moment – to make the most of each and every day. I am glad I was able to share that with my readers. I will never wish my life away again.

I can't wait for tomorrow and the election. As I write this sentence, the first poll will close in 33 hours and twenty-two minutes. I was going to give the seconds, but they kept changing on me. I am so nervous and excited and impatient that...that I have to do something to make the time seem to go by faster.

By the way, here I am, waiting for this election to end, and you know what I had to do this weekend? I had to set my clock BACK one hour. One entire hour. Unbelievable.

So I'm waiting again, and The Kinks are singing in my head, and I've decided to relive the Greatest Hits of 2008 election so that time will pass and The Kinks will shut up. I was going to write something about working The Kinks out, but I decided against it.

The single greatest hit of this election cycle (which sounds like a washing machine) is the boom it was for *Saturday Night Live* in general and Tina Fey in particular. Thanks for finding the humor.

Diddly Squat provided two classics from my perspective. He continued to say that he would follow Bin Laden to the four corners of the earth. I was hoping Obama would lean over and say, "Ah, excuse me, but we have decent evidence now that supports the notion that the world is round, and therefore doesn't actually have corners..." Of course that didn't happen, but wouldn't it have been funny if it had?

The other good one was McCain's constant use of, "You know, there's a reason I didn't win Miss Congeniality." I wanted to reply, "Yes – and the reason is that you are a man." Unless...You don't think...No...Forget that.

Joe Biden put his foot in his mouth with his, "Obama will be tested" comments. Way to help your running mate, Joe.

Crazy preachers spiced things up. (They used garlic and paprika). And every person who ever had a political opinion, with the exception of my wife and me, got to express it on one network or another. It seems the one thing all networks are expert on is speculation.

Speculation has become the major operation of every network – except Fox News. Fox News gets its info. directly from God, so there is no speculation there, only the gospel of prophets like Hannity and O'Reilly.

People have waited four, six, eight, even ten hours to vote, and that's during early voting. I wonder if tomorrow will be complete chaos. I wonder if we'll know early, or have to wait for days or weeks or months. I wonder if I've got enough Rolling Rock™.

I have already read an article speculating on the frontrunners for 2012. Of course, who is the frontrunner depends on who actually wins this election, but that was taken into account in the article.

Meanwhile, I continue to wait. I'm *Waiting for Godot,* waiting for the bus, for my ship to come in. It's the waiting game. I guess that makes me a waiter. "May I take your order please? Do you want fries with that?"

Just you wait – I can't wait. Wait a minute, I think...Why wait? Hurry up and wait. This election has got to end. It better be worth the wait.

Chapter IX. – Election Eve Part II
Or: Wait a Minute

It is evening – 22 hours until the first poll closes. And, as if there isn't enough drama in my life, a football coach I respect, the leader of my favorite team, the University of Tennessee, is forced to resign on election eve.

Phillip Fulmer has won 75 percent of his games – and a National Championship. He has had a few rough seasons recently. In the, "What have you done for me lately" world of college football, loyalty does not matter.

At the press conference, Fulmer was quite emotional. I've never seen anyone look more hurt (unless it was at a funeral). It appeared that his heart had been crushed. His players vacillated between hurt and anger. I wanted to tell him, "Don't worry Phil – you can now be a fired SEC coach with a huge buyout and ESPN expert potential. You can sit with Kurt and Lee and make fun of those still coaching." But that wouldn't have made him feel better.

The guy played at UT. He coached there in many different capacities before becoming the head coach. Isn't head coach a curious phrase? How come no other body parts get a coach? It is football, so why isn't there a foot coach? Wait, there is a tight ends' coach, but I'm pretty sure that refers to a position on the field, not the body. And if an ugly person can be pretty sure of something, can a pretty person be ugly sure of something?

Jocularity aside, Phillip Fulmer spent four decades at UT. He donated $1,000,000 to the school – and now he's done. A disgruntled fan base -- especially some influential boosters -- is the primary culprit. There may be another dickweed chapter in my future.

And Phillip Fulmer's forced resignation is only one of the terrible election eve occurrences. Barack Obama's grandmother – the woman who helped to raise and guide a presidential aspirant, did not live to see the outcome. She died the day before, and I can't think of too many things sadder than that.

Both of these events were not surprises. Talk radio had been predicting Fulmer's demise for months. In the case of the presidential hopeful, he left the campaign for several days to visit his grandmother because her health was so bad. So neither event was a surprise, but both events sucked the joy out of the evening.

I just mentioned talk radio, and I think that is an appropriate term for what goes on, even if the radio doesn't actually talk. The hosts and the callers talk – and talk – and talk – and say very little. Maybe we need listen radio – or better yet, think radio. I'm not betting the ranch on that. Of course I don't own a ranch – if I did it would be a dude ranch – but if I did own one, I wouldn't bet it on talk radio becoming thoughtful.

That's all I wanted to say. I don't intend to write another word until I know who the president-elect is. I wish this book could talk, and that we could cue up Walter Cronkite's voice, and he would say, "And that's the way it is – Monday, November 3rd, 2008." I seem to have written a bunch of words without knowing who the president-elect is. I am sorry, and I will stop, as soon as I ask, "Do words come in bunches?" Okay, I'm done.

Chapter XX. – YEESSSSS!!!
Or: YEESSSSS!!!

On Tuesday, November 4th, a minute or two after 11:00 p.m. (Eastern Time) Barack Obama became the 44th President of the United States. Technically, he became President-elect, but who cares. I was there – Rolling Rock™ in hand and Tim Russert in my heart – to watch history unfold. And I'm not going to play silly games with the word unfold, because BARACK OBAMA WON!!!

A black man was elected president. It seemed as if the whole world was watching – and hoping – and celebrating. I know that's not true, but that's how it felt.

And, because I am so happy, and because Senator McCain gave such an eloquent concession speech, I am not going to call him Diddly Squat anymore. Elections make me do mature things.

President Obama. Hail to the Chief – The Commander-in-Chief. To quote that great poet and philosopher Fred Flintstone, "Yabba Dabba Do!"

The post election analysis has already begun, but I'm going to do something no other pundit or expert will do. I'm going to tell you the real reason Barack Obama won. He won because he got more votes. Okay, that's pathetic, but let me now tell you why he got more votes.

Unbeknownst to this author, a third major event took place on election eve. I was totally unaware of this event until Election Day, so that is why it was not included in the election eve chapter. This event has gone from being unbeknownst to fully beknownst now – and the ramifications are…well…it won the white house.

Monday Night Football was on T.V., because, well, it was Monday night. I usually don't watch *MNF* because I prefer the college game and *MNF* ends past my bedtime. Plus, after watching U.T. lose again, when Hank Williams, Jr. asked, "Are you ready for some football?" I answered, "No."

However, *MNF* had an interview with both presidential candidates. Both were asked to identify an area related to sports that he would like to change. Diddly Squat (remember he hadn't given his concession speech at that point) talked about steroids and their terrible impact on sports. A good answer. A truly important aspect, but nothing when compared to what his opponent said. Candidate Obama said that NCAA division one football needs a playoff, just like all the other sports. He'd pick eight teams and decide the issue on the field. No more BCS.

I'm sure voters across America took notice. I'm sure there were some who voted for John McCain during the early voting period. I am sure that they slapped their forehead, ala, "I could have had a V-8™," and maybe even kicked themselves for wasting their vote. I wish I could have seen the actual kicking, but that wasn't possible.

It is my belief that numerous previously undecided voters immediately became decided. It is hard to estimate how big a role this played in the outcome, but if Obama had campaigned on this issue from the start, he would have won an electoral landslide. I know, he did win an electoral landslide. But it could have been an even bigger landslide. If football crazy Texas and Oklahoma had known…forget it. In fact, it could have been a shut-out, except for Alaska, but we'll never know.

I fully expect that, no later than January 31st, an executive order will be issued mandating a college football playoff. Obama will have a 94 percent approval rating, the Taliban will know they are dealing with a serious leader and subsequently surrender, the stock market will soar, and peace will break out across the Middle East.

He can fix health care and global warming during the second week. But, in the unlikely event that things don't turn out this way, I am still happy, because America has a president who:

A) Speaks in complete sentences
B) Is liked by other countries
C) Has read the Constitution
D) Wants a college football playoff
E) Can pronounce nuclear
F) Doesn't smirk
G) Wants a college football playoff
H) Isn't you know who.

And then there was Grant Park, and Oprah's tears, and old black women and young white women, little boys and girls of all colors, and I have rarely if ever been so moved. I wonder how many gallons of happy tears – joyful tears – tears of relief and hope and pride were shed that night. My wife and I were happy to contribute our share, and I still missed Tim Russert, and I went to bed later and happier than usual, and all was right in the world. Bring on the playoffs.

Chapter XXI. – Back Asswords
Or: No Behind Left to a Child

Suppose I told you about a school system that said in order to graduate, a student had to be able to dunk a basketball. Ridiculous, right? In the words of Lee Corso, "Not so fast, my friend."

Bear with me – but keep your clothes on. I guess that would be bare with me – but that's a different chapter. Do we have a right to bear arms or to bare arms? Or both? Black bear or grizzly bear? I may have digressed here.

So a school randomly picks one area in which students much demonstrate proficiency in order to graduate. Instead of chemistry, School X picks dunking. Their logic? None. Logic is not required when selecting a standard for measuring students, although there is probably some board of education member arguing that people make more money dunking than they do using the Periodic Table.

So now everyone at School X has to dunk. We have raised the bar, but not the good kind that serves alcohol. The school begins to teach to the physical test. Rigorous training is instituted. The fact that some students simply can't perform the task is irrelevant. The fact that some non-performers are wonderful human beings with other, unmeasurable talents is ignored. Students will dunk OR ELSE. If the school will only work harder, no dunker will be left behind.

Except there are those who can't dunk. When it finally occurs to School X, or the school board, or the politicians who helped enact such legislation that many students won't graduate, panic sets in. A tsunami of parental complaints begins. There is only one solution. It is decided that students still must dunk – but they can use a nine foot basket. Lowering the bar (but not the good kind) raises the number who can dunk, but there are still non-dunkers in the school. What to do?

Specialists are hired. Tutorials are given. And still, four foot eleven inch Sally Ledbottom can't dunk. More meetings – more revisions – an eight and-a-half foot goal, and Sally tries her best, and she is getting closer, but she still can't do it. That's when the trampoline becomes part of the equation, and Sally dunks and everyone involved congratulates each other for raising the standards at School X.

When I was a kid, we had an expression for someone we thought was weak. We'd say, "He can't fight his way out of a paper bad." If he was real weak, we'd make it a wet paper bag.

Just like there are, "Can't carry his jock strap" equivalents, there are paper bag equivalents as well. I believe the laws regulating student achievement are made by administrators and politicians who cannot teach their way out of a paper bag.

Let's start with a premise: All people need to pass the same test or possess the same skills. If we accept that premise, everything else follows. I'm not talking about basic reading or math, of course everyone needs that. But I have my doubts about chemistry or dunking or algebra. Not for those non-college bound students who will fight our wars, fix our cars, grow our food, style our hair, build our bridges, and pave our roads. In other words – the majority – the backbone – the people who will work with their hands and build America.

There exists, in our country, a prejudice no one ever discusses. It isn't as damaging as racial and sexual bigotry, or as hateful. But it is equally stupid.

It is what I call a "two-way" prejudice – two groups equally narrow-minded. In its simplest form, it's the athletes who hate the academic achievers and the academics who put down "dumb jocks." Only this goes a little deeper. College educated people who work with their minds should know better, but I swear some of them look down their noses at "common laborers." Of course looking down your nose is dangerous – especially if you are walking or, worse, driving. And there is nothing common about the incredible skills our laborers possess.

And there are many workers who think doctors and lawyers and teachers aren't "the workin' man" because they use their minds and their "product" is harder to measure. We need to respect each other's talents – we are better than that. And we need to keep that in mind when we randomly decide what kids need to master.

One size does not fit all. But we keep teaching like it does – and we keep letting politicians who could never teach their way out of a wet paper bag dictate policy. And a talk show host who dropped out of college his freshman year is a poor mouthpiece for those people to use – as if he is some educational guru.

Some of my gentle and ungentle readers may view this chapter as me venting. To those people I say, "Yeah – so?" I like the term venting. I like to vent. See Ray vent. Vent Ray, vent. Vent here Ray. Good venting.

Of course, the problem is the language. Pass a law. Call it No Child Left Behind. How could any person not approve of that? Do you want to leave children behind? Are you heartless?

In America, it is important to have the correct title. Gems such as The Patriot Act, The Clean Air Act, The Clean Water Act, and the NCAA Football Playoff Act are so well-phrased they can't be defeated, no matter what they actually accomplish. I tried to slip the Playoff Act in there just to see who was paying attention. But when President Obama gets around to it (the day after inauguration day), I suggest he find a better way to phrase the act. Perhaps:

- The No Team Left Out Playoff Act, or
- The Fair Play Playoff Act, or
- The Equal Opportunity Playoff Act, or
- The Patriotic Playoff Act, or
- The God-given Right to a Playoff Act, or
- The Anti-Communism Playoff Act, or
- The Homeland Security Playoff Act

There. I am all vented out. I feel better, and I hope America does, also.

Chapter XXII. – Still More Dickweeds Or: The Beat Goes On

I'm not sure if there is a hell or not, but if there is, I hope there's a special wing for the following dickweeds:

- Litterers
- Bigots
- People who make promises they had no intention of keeping
- People who ruin movie endings
- People who talk through movies
- People who will talk to you about their problems for hours, but won't spend any time listening to yours
- People who feel it's their mission to convert you to whatever it is they believe
- People who make fun of anyone with a physical or mental problem
- Con artists who prey on the elderly
- Athletes who don't respect the game
- Teachers who hate kids
- Fans who boo amateur athletes
- Parents who are obnoxious, frustrated former athletes (or at least think they are) and make little league hell for all concerned.

Most of these things aren't illegal. A few are. I'm not talking about the obvious – the felons -- the murderers and molesters and rapists. I'm talking about people who are the jock-itch of life. If only there was a spray to relieve us from their form of infestation. And the hits just keep on coming, like:

- Salesmen (and women) who learn your name and use it in every freakin' sentence
- Kids who think they should be allowed to sleep in class
- Parents who fight their children's battles because their precious child could not possibly be wrong – ever
- People who think tears are a sign of weakness
- People who refuse to apologize – no matter how wrong they are
- Rich boosters who break rules and codes of ethics in the hope of landing prized recruits for their college or university
- Alabama fans (although that is somewhat redundant)
- People who get wasted at concerts and sporting events and ruin the event for others.

I am sure that my dear, amazing friend Sheryl – remember Sheryl? She inspired this book...I'm sure she would agree with this assessment of the dickweeds among us. It is my firm belief that once she receives her personally autographed copy of this book, she will be moved to ask, "Isn't personally autographed redundant? Can you impersonally autograph something? Isn't an autograph always done personally?" And then, after dealing with those issues, she will be inspired to write a song about the dickweeds among us. She might call it *Dickweeds Among Us*, or *Ode to Dickweeds*, or maybe *The Dickweed Blues*. She will, no doubt, dedicate the song to me, not because I'm a dickweed, but because of my brilliant exposé of dickweed behavior – a tristice of dickweediness so to speak. I wonder if the word dickweediness has ever been written before, and if so, by whom? And why?

I can't wait for the song. I hope it has a catchy tune and deep images and metaphors. I hope it soars to number one on the charts, and I hope Sheryl shares her royalties with me.

Chapter XXIII. – Post Election Stress Disorder
Or: Bar the Door Jethro – They're Comin' for Our Guns

It has been eighteen days since the historic election of '08. President Bush is still the President, there is no college football play-off, the economy sucks, and speculation runs rampant about who will serve in which cabinet position. I have not yet been approached, but I'm sure Secretary of Education is in my future. Which brings up two questions. The first is why do things like speculation always run rampant? Why don't they ever walk or jog or trot rampant? And secondly, why do these people who head major aspects of government get the title of secretary? And thirdly (I know I said it brought up two questions – now I'm on number three – deal with it) do these secretaries have secretaries? Is there a person who is the Energy Secretary's secretary?

That's not what this chapter is about. I just threw that in as an added bonus (not to be confused with a subtracted bonus). Aren't all bonuses added on to something – isn't that what makes it a bonus? I didn't really throw it in there, either – I just wrote it.

I really want to write about an amazing post-election phenomenon, so I will. In the midst of a terrible recession, with bail-outs occurring faster than Hollywood marriages, one element of our economy has surged. I am speaking of the gun industry.

Reports indicate, "A spike in their sales," which sounds painful, or, "Sales going through the roof," which sounds dangerous, but whatever the cliché, people are stocking up on guns. Why? "Because that Obama feller is gonna take our guns."

That's right ladies and gentlemen; the great gun round-up is coming. Get ready.

I wonder how these deep thinkers have escaped their own dickweed chapter. I wonder what other rumors stir them up? I wonder if stirring them up is a good phrase for what happens in their heads – like some cosmic chief is pouring in varying ingredients of stupidity and using a mixer to blend it all in.

I wonder how they picture this happening. Suddenly, there is a loud knock on the door. Joe GunOwner (cousin of Joe Sixpack and Joe the Plumber) opens his door and finds a black man surrounded by F.B.I. agents with guns drawn. The man says, "Hi – I'm Barack Obama, and I'm here for your guns." With the help of the agents, the house is searched, the guns are confiscated, and the posse moseys on down the road to the next unsuspecting, law-abiding citizen.

Of course, this is a time-consuming process. With all the gun owners in America, it would take President Obama 322 years, but that's a minor detail. "He's gonna take our guns."

Forget the fact that gun ownership was never mentioned in the presidential debates. Forget the little detail that the president does not have the power to do that. (Besides, he will be too busy working on the college football playoff). Forget the fact that Obama has taught Constitutional law and believes that the second amendment protects individual ownership. Let's just focus in (or take aim – since it's guns) on the logic at work here.

I – Joe GunOwner – believe someone is coming for my guns, SO I BUY NEW ONES!! I don't want 'em takin' my old stuff – gotta get new ones.

I know – maybe they're going to hide them, or maybe they're really worried about restrictions on future sales, or bans on the manufacture of certain weapons. That may be true, but all I ever hear in Red State Tennessee is, "He's gonna take our guns."

Personally, I think President Obama will be too busy being the socialist Muslim Anti-Christ to worry about guns, but I could be wrong.

Nothing stands stronger than a misconception rooted in ignorance. My teen-agers pass this information around almost as fast as, "Who's doin' it with whom" rumors – although they never use whom. "My daddy said so – it must be true. I read it on the internet – it must be true."

I've decided there is only one logical way to combat this. I tell them, "He don't care 'bout your guns – he's too busy eatin' babies." The conversation about guns stops immediately. This new-found knowledge about Barack the Baby Eater is too good to pass up. They want to know how many, and when, and how come they didn't know about it, and so many other juicy tidbits of information (which is a disgusting choice of words that I hope my editor fixes). Some are skeptical. Some are relieved he's not after their guns – a few babies is a small sacrifice for keeping your rocket launcher. The lesson about how easy it is to start rumors resonates with approximately 38.77% of the class. The rest are too anxious for the bell to ring so they can pass on their latest information. Some of them are on their way to lucrative careers at Fox News.

Personally, I think there is a lesson here. If a rumor about Obama confiscating guns helps the "gun economy," why not use that it other areas? If it were me, I'd start more rumors. For example, "That Obama feller wants to take our hybrid cars." Boom! A rush on the hybrid car market. Or, "That Obama feller wants to outlaw General Motors." Immediately GM is saved. No bail-out required.

I have many other ideas that will save the country – but I'll just wait for the cabinet meeting to share them. I've got to go buy me an Uzi.

Chapter XXIV. – One More Serious One Or: I Miss Him, Too

Tim Russert wasn't the only recent death that made me sad. George Carlin is no longer alive, and that stinks.

I loved Carlin. No one has ever been more insightful, more astute – especially about words. I'd like to think he would have enjoyed my take on the Curmudgeon Virgins – so I will. He sure had his share of battles with "those types."

Say Carlin's name and people immediately start hearing the seven words you can't say on television. Me too – but that's just one small part of his genius. There are all those characters – from Al Sleet (the hippie dippy weatherman) to the DJ from Wonderful WINO. There was baseball vs. football, and "My Stuff," and some of the best political satire ever. He captured ethnicity in the city, Catholic guilt, and Wall Street greed.

But he is known for THOSE WORDS. And his ranting that someone, somewhere, got to decide that there are bad words – Baadd Woordds – BAAD WOORRDS!! There are also dirty words, filthy words, disgusting, wash your mouth out with soap or you will go to hell words. And after talking about them, he would say them – each and every one, and pointing out our Puritanical silliness and prudishness in the process.

He made me think. Sure, he made me laugh, and that's a powerful gift, but while he was being outrageously funny, he had a point to make. He filled me with wonder – and I am grateful for that – and in awe of his talents. And thanks to the miracle of audio and video tape, he will never be silenced. But even if those things didn't exist, he would still sound as loud and clear and funny as the first time I heard him, because he has a permanent gig in my head and perpetual humor in my heart.

Thanks George – you still rock – even after death. How many people can you say that about?

Chapter XXV. – Full Disclosure
Or: True Confessions

I feel that all of my gentle readers – and most of my ungentle ones – are entitled to some information that some writers – lesser writers no doubt – just might not share. So I am going to "fess up," lay it on the line, come clean. I have no idea what line I am laying it on, or where the line is, but I'm going to do it anyway. Coming clean sounds…well…it sounds cleansing and refreshing – or perverted, depending on your outlook. If people don't "fess up," are they laying it off the line? Coming dirty? It boggles the mind.

Boggles sounds like a game show. Or a fruit drink. Or sexy undergarments. "Did you see that model in her skimpy boggles? Whoa, baby."

The purpose of this chapter is not to engage in mindless word-play or immature, sexual innuendo. That's just a pleasant side-effect. The purpose is to admit that I haven't written ANY STINKIN' THING in almost two months!

There it is: full disclosure. Not partial disclosure, nor unfull disclosure, but honest to badness full disclosure. True confessions. Aren't all confessions supposed to be true? Wouldn't an untrue confession defeat the purpose?

If one watches a movie, one gets the illusion that it was filmed in sequence – start to finish. Intellectually, one may know that it was filmed out of sequence, often over long periods of time, but the editing process creates the appearance of a seamless shooting. One, or two or three for that matter, never notices the glitches or delays. So it is with all great works of art – including this epic.

Why have I been remiss is my writing? I will tell you. First, there was the accident. My wonderful vehicle – the one with the political bumper sticker – was T-boned – struck down – crashed into. I never saw it coming. The other car came completely out of the red and…Pow – Boom – Twisted metal and deployed air bags and nastiness galore.

I know some may question my statement that the other car came out of the red. They might ask, "Aren't unseen things supposed to come out of the blue?"

I reply, "Au contraire." Actually, I wouldn't use that specific phrase, but that would be my meaning.

Why did blue get such a bad rap? Why don't things ever come out of the green? Or purple?

I live in a red state. The dickweed in the other vehicle ran a red light. He came out of the red. No one was hurt, but his van was totaled and my truck was badly injured. For 65 days – let me repeat that – for 65 freakin' days I did not have my truck. I was left to hope that my political bumper sticker would not influence the care my vehicle received. It appears that it did not.

I had the joys of rental cars and police reports and insurance agencies to deal with. New dickweed chapters seemed to spring up from everywhere.

In addition, the accident occurred at the end of the semester. I had exams and grades to deal with – or with which to deal if you are a descendant of the Curmudgeon Virgins and can't abide ending a sentence with a preposition (which I also did in the last paragraph).

And then there were the holiday seasons – Thanksgiving, Christmas, and New Years. There was also a heat pump problem and a, "Hey – it's New Year's morning and we don't have any water" issue. I hope that's not an omen.

So I lost my writing mojo (whatever the hell that is). But now I seem to have it – and my truck is all better – and a new semester has begun. There are new teen-agers to laugh with. There is heat and water aplenty. And during all this time, during two months of chaos, Barack Obama is still not in the White House. But he will be, in eight more days, and I will write with more regularity, which sounds like I was communicatively constipated, and that may be accurate, but now all will be right with the world, except for the dickweeds among us who come out of the red and wreck things, but we shall overcome, and this may be the longest sentence I have ever written, so I'm going to stop now and let you come up for oxygen. Happy New Year.

Chapter XXVI. – Christmas Shopping Or: Deck This

During my writing hiatus, I experienced the joys of the holiday season. Those joys included a major controversy about the use of the words "Happy Holidays" instead of "Merry Christmas." It included decorating and shopping and eating and drinking and exchanging presents and eating and drinking.

I went to the mall – once. I try to do most of my shopping online (presumably the same line I used to lay it on the line in the last chapter). I certainly was smart enough to avoid the Black Friday hoard. I went early one morning. The mall was almost empty – just me and the Mall Walkers. I was strolling through the decked halls when I came upon an empty kiosk that said, "Dippin' Dots – The Ice cream of the Future." Actually the kiosk didn't speak, but the sign above it had those words on it. I wasn't taken aback, because I stood in one place, but I was…interested. I mean, how often do you get to see the future? That's when I smiled. Then I chuckled. I did, I chuckled right there in the mall. I chuckled because it occurred to me that the ice cream of the future has been around for a very long time. In fact, Dippin' Dots is old news. I wished someone had been manning the booth, or womanning the booth, because I wanted to ask how old the company of the future was.

Unfortunately, no one was there. I guess people don't do ice cream early in the morning. I went on to other stores, purchasing gifts for my friends and relations. But every once-in-awhile, I thought of Dippin' Dots and it brought a smile to my face.

Then people started to show up. Lines formed, children cried, people got pushy and grumpy and I'd had enough Christmas spirit for one day, so I left. I was going to go home and research the history of the ice cream of the future, but I was distracted and never got around to it. But I do wonder – how many years can you claim to be the ice cream of the future before you look silly doing so?

There is a commercial on T.V. for a company (which I refuse to name) that wants people who owe the government $10,000-$20,000-$100,000 or more in unpaid taxes. Their claim is that they will settle the claim for a fraction of what is really owed. Then a person or a couple testifies about how wonderful said company is. A typical statement from Joe the Dickweed or JoAnn the Deadbeat might be, "We owed the I.R.S. $85,000, but thanks to said company, we settled our bill for $29.95." Then you see the smiling couple – all happy and proud – having just ripped off the taxpayers who actually pay their taxes. My wife hates this commercial. I hate it, also.

How is this legal? Why is the I.R.S. so kind to those people and so tough on others? With our debt and our deficit exploding, how can this happen? I mention it because, during the holiday season, I saw this commercial more often than the dorky commercials for the car with a humongous red bow on it. Nothing gets a man into the holiday spirit like watching a smug, happy couple basking in the glory of not paying their taxes.

And while I was being inundated with all kinds of crappy Christmas commercials, the classics were mysteriously absent. Tradition was shot to hell – spirits were dashed. Here is an example of America's moral decay – a decline in our nation's spirit. I speak of the saddest of events. This holiday season (which I think started in August) ended with Zero – Nada – not one Clapper™ commercial. Let me reiterate – no "Clap On." No "Clap Off." Is nothing sacred? Just red bows on cars and I.R.S. rip-offs.

And that's not all. There was another American icon missing – A.W.O.L. – non-existent. Where – in the name of all that is patriotic – was the Chia Pet™? How is a person supposed to deck the halls or sleep in heavenly peace or think about joy to the world without a little, "Cha, Cha, Cha, Chia" in his life?

I wonder if that Obama feller took 'em. I'll bet he did.

I interrupt this chapter for some late-breaking news. The cabinet is set. I do not have a position – no Secretary of Education, no Commerce, not even Interior. What in the hell does an Interior Secretary do? Deck the halls? Pick out placemats? And how come we don't have an Exterior Secretary? Maybe that's it – the future president is going to create a new Department of the Exterior, and that's when I get the call.

I'm sorry for that interruption. I wish that just once there would be early breaking news. And I'm sorry that the flow of my Christmas season ranting was broken by political concerns.

Let's review. Dippin' Dots has been, continues to be, and will remain the ice cream of the future. Tax evaders are glorified, even during the holiday season. The Clapper™ and the Chia Pet™ are no longer an integral part of our lives. President-elect Obama has more to address than I thought.

Oh, and a final Christmas thought. In America, people can say, "Merry Christmas," or "Happy Holidays," or "Season's Greetings," or "Shuck a Monkey" if they want to. And people need to get over their own righteous indignation about it (with the possible exception of shucking the monkey). So there! Merry Happy Seasons Holiday Christmas Greetings to ya'll.

Chapter XXVII. – Here We Go Again
Or: Come In From the Cold

It's that time of year again. That time when the weather changes faster than an Obama gun round-up. One day it will be 70°, and Spring Fever is percolating. I believe the percolation begins in the small intestine, but I could be wrong. And just when you're breaking out the shorts and sandals – BAM! 12° -- ice, wind, and snow. Then it turns 70 again, followed by thunderstorms and tornado warnings, then – BAM! 12° again.

This phenomenon is not new, but it guarantees three predictable and stupid things will happen.

First, people will swear that this is the craziest weather they have ever seen. It does not matter that they have said that dozens of times before. It does not matter that they said it last year. All that matters is THIS time it is, by far, the craziest weather in the history of the universe. That's not a huge social problem, just a weird trait of our less than logical population.

The second guaranteed behavior is the expressed belief that no other place on Earth has weather as unpredictable as the place where I live. Since I live in East Tennessee, I'll hear, "Well – that's East Tennessee weather for ya'. Just the craziest weather there is."

Of course, they say that in Chicago, and Florida, and Montana, and New Jersey, and Outer Mongolia. (Okay, I can't swear to Outer Mongolia, but I'll bet they do). So what does that prove? It proves that people don't travel much for one thing. It proves that people say the same boring clichés all over the world for another. And it proves that we don't have much to talk about for yet another. Not that this is a huge social problem either.

But it does bring us to the third guaranteed behavior, and this one is a huge social issue.

Every time, and I do mean each and every single time, without fail, every time there is bad weather there is some poor man or woman who must expose himself or herself to the elements so that the dumbasses watching at home can understand that there is bad weather outside. I don't mean that they literally expose themselves to the elements, as in taking off their clothes (although it might make for some entertaining viewing). I mean that the reporter/meteorologist/person who drew the short straw has to go outside and get pummeled by the weather he or she is telling everyone to avoid. WHY?

It's two degrees outside. The wind is howling. Snow is falling faster than the stock market. The anchorman/woman is all warm and cozy in the studio, warning the listeners not to go outside or they will die. Then he/she cuts to Donald Dimwit who is up to his butt in snow. He can barely stand the wind is so strong. He has to shout over the noise. He screams, "It's a mess out here. Visibility is maybe 10 feet. The snow is coming down sideways – and drifts are forming along the road." Then he'll show us a thermometer that reads two degrees, he'll almost lose his balance, he'll tell us how cold and miserable he is, then he'll "throw" it back to the toasty anchorman/woman, who will tell him to be careful and come in out of the cold. This is considered fine, cutting edge reporting. Although I'm not sure what edge is being cut, I am sure that every freaking network in America uses this idiotic technique – and the fact that they all use it tells me it must be successful, which tells me that American television audiences are either sadistic or totally lacking in imagination. By the way, the poor camera person is out there also, getting no valuable air time but still freezing his/her butt off. America's highways are littered with butts that have been frozen off of camera people. Think of that the next time you hit what you thought was a speed bump.

Wouldn't it be nice to find a network/ station/ news organization that didn't send its reporters outside in the terrible weather? I swear I would immediately switch to that station. Maybe they could use one of the quadrillion file films they have and say, "This is Hurricane Horatio pounding Naples, Florida two years ago. See how the weather person can hardly stand? See all the trees bending and debris flying and rain coming down sideways? Our current Hurricane, Penelope, looks just like that only it's pounding coastal Texas. And we are not sending another human being out into a storm ever again. And if you somehow feel ripped off because nobody from our station is risking life and limb to show you want you've seen hundreds of times before, then you need to find some roller derby to watch – or some mud wrestlin'.

Can't they just stick a camera out a window? Wouldn't you love to hear a weather person say, "Look out your window. See how crappy it is outside? It's just like that here, too. Why don't we all stay inside until this blows over?"

It is sad when we can't even be logical about reporting the weather. I wonder if the war correspondents began as weather reporters, only to seek newer, more dangerous thrills. I wonder why people being attacked by domestic falling trees are called reporters and people dodging foreign bullets are called correspondents. I wonder who the first person was who said, "Look how bad this weather is -- we need someone to go outside." But most of all, I wonder why we keep watching this silly exercise in irrationality. What would George Carlin say?

Chapter XXVIII. – Stained Steel
Or: Truth in Advertising

Clinton, Tennessee. My home town – a town of banks, drug stores, pawn shops, and more antique shops per capita than any place I have ever been. And tobacco shops. In fact, in South Clinton, (not to be confused with non-existent North or East or West Clinton) is a tobacco shop called *Smoke and Croak*. Honest.

Is that not the greatest name ever? Talk about truth in advertising, there it is. *Smoke and Croak*.

My son pointed that out to me. I had been oblivious – just riding by without noticing the name. Now, I laugh every time I go by it.

Makes me long for other truthful enterprises, like a liquor store named *Chug and Hurl* or a gun shop called *Aim and Maim* or barbecue shop called *Hog and (Artery) Clog*. Okay, that last one is a little awkward, but you get the idea.

I just purchased a new charcoal grill – a Perfect Flame™ charcoal grill to be exact. I like it, even though page 14 of the instruction manual contains the following words: *"To remove the stains on the stainless steel lid and front panel caused by fumigation while grilling, use of a cleaning pad is recommended."*

Yup, that's what it said, and I am a better person for knowing how to remove stains from a STAINLESS STEEL – STAINLESS

STEEL – STAINLESS FREAKIN' STEEL grill. And now, so do you. Use a cleaning pad.

And that's not the only thing that bothers me. What in the hell is the deal with the word "fumigation?" Don't you fumigate places that are crawling with germs? What's that got to do with me grilling some burgers? I just want my readers to know that I am vigilant -- I am relentless – I will not allow fumigation induced stains to form on my stainless steel – not so long as there is a breath in my body or a cleaning pad in my fist.

The same page also advises: *"Most surfaces are hot when in use."* Thanks for that news bulletin. Makes you wonder what kind of burn/ lawsuit/ disaster made the grill people feel a need to spell out the obvious. You know some dumbass did something incredibly stupid while the grill was hot, causing the Perfect Flame™ people to engage in cover your ass language. I am thankful that:

A) asses are being covered
B) people are being protected from themselves
C) my college education made me fully aware of the need not to place my hand on a hot grill.

I wonder if the dumbasses who necessitated the warning are the same ones who:

A) need to see the weather person being clobbered by the hurricane
B) feed fish next to a sign that tells them not to
C) think that Obama feller is gonna take their guns.

Maybe I need to research this. Maybe I'll stop in at the *Smoke and Croak* or the *Aim and Maim* and take a poll. Or maybe I'll just stay home and polish my stainless steel grill.

Chapter XXIX. – Uncommon Stuff
Or: Imperfections

I have some early breaking news. Members of the medical community believe they are close to a cure for the common cold. The uncommon cold? Not so close, but the common one? Yessireee Bob. I have no idea who Bob is or why he gets added to yessiree, but he does. I am tempted to make something up, but I may have done that a time or three in earlier chapters, so I will skip that juvenile behavior and continue.

Bob Marley was such a hero in his native land that every time he said something, people agreed because they knew it would be correct. Yes sir became yessiree, and, because of Bob Marley and his Rastafarian ways – and perhaps because of weed, it quickly because yessiree Bob.

But back to the medical community's hope of curing the common cold. I say, "Right on medical community! Way to go!"

Doesn't "medical community" sound like a commune somewhere in North Dakota? I'll bet they're out there in the Bad Lands. Or is the Bad Lands in South Dakota? And should that be, "Or <u>are</u> the Bad Lands in South Dakota?" And should Bad Lands be one word – like dickweed? Does it need to be capitalized? And why are they so bad? Are there any Good Lands? Or goodlands? My mind is now completely boggled. I think the medical community, after they cure the common cold, should find a cure for boggled minds. "Take two unbogglers and call me in the morning."

Which brings me to perfect strangers. How many times have people used those words?

John: Do you like Penelope?

Frank: Penelope who?

John: Why, Penelope Lipschitz.

Frank: I have no idea who that is.

John: You don't know Penelope?

Frank: That's what I just said.

John: I thought you knew her.

Frank: Nope – we're perfect strangers.

We interrupt this scintillating conversation because it has served its purpose. No its purpose was not to bore the hell out of you. And I have no idea who "we" refers to, since Sheryl is not writing this with me. But I do know that for Frank to say that he and Penelope Lipshitz are perfect strangers is exactly the way we all talk. I think it is presumptuous at best and slightly egotistical at worst. But if Frank had said, "Nope – we're imperfect strangers," people would look at Frank like he's weird – even though he might be correct. Sort of like Galileo and that pesky solar system stuff. Okay, maybe not exactly the same, but close enough. Close enough for what? I have no idea.

Chapter XXX. – Corporate America
Or: The Grass is Greener

So far, I have read every chapter of this epic to my lovely and talented wife, Cindy. I have read them to her because she can't read. Ha ha ha. Keep in mind, I am going to read that last sentence to her, and I'm not sure she will be pleased. What I should have said is, I have read every chapter to her because she can't read my writing. Nobody can. Plus, she gets the advantage of hearing my voice – kind of like her personal book on tape. My wife is one lucky woman.

Astute readers may be observing, "He writes his book longhand instead of on a computer? How old-fashioned." That is correct astute readers, I write all of my stuff longhand, even though my hands are on the short or small size. The extremely astute readers are saying, "Just like Chaucer and Shakespeare." Thank you, extremely astute readers.

The reason I write things out is because my typing skills are… well…I am to typing what Dick Cheney is to hunter safety – Fox is to News – What impeached Rod Blagojevich is to ethical government. By the way, that little twit just signed a six figure agreement to write a book about his dishonesty. Who says crime doesn't pay? Am I bitter? Yes.

I am one speedy writer. I am messy, but quick, and I fully expect corporate America to become part of this process. I have written every word of this book with a Pilot™ precise grip pen. I have written on Oak Ridge Office Supply yellow legal pad. Technically, the color is called canary, but who cares? I will not be surprised if, upon publication, this book is called *The Pilot Pen™ Search for Diddly Squat (or: The Oak Ridge Office Supply's Mall Walker's Guide to the Universe)*.

Which brings me to twitter. That's right – twitter. I'm not sure I had ever heard of this activity until President Obama gave a speech to a joint session of Congress. Who decided to call it a "joint session?" Is that not the greatest name ever? No wonder politicians spend so much money to get elected. They get to go to joint sessions. In fact, judging by some of the things our Congress people have done, I'd say they've been to a few too many joint sessions.

Maybe that explains why, at the last joint session, certain members of Congress broke into twittering. Yup – they did – right there in front of anyone watching the speech. Novices like me assumed they were texting. But no – we were informed by "those in the know," certain media types, that they were not texting. They were twittering. During the President's speech. I believe those who twitter under such circumstances must be twits. I'll bet Blagojevich twitters like crazy.

In school, their twittering devices would be confiscated and they would get detention. Bad Congress people. Rude Congress people.

One of the things that bothers me is the fact that an entire group of people was twittering away while the rest of us naïvely led twitterless lives. We did not know what we were missing. Some of us still don't, and don't care, but that is not the point here. I'm no longer sure exactly what the point is here, but I know that's not it.

Wait – I do know the point. The point is that out Congress is full of twittering dickweeds hoping to be impeached or censured or somehow involved in a scandal so they can sign a six-figure book deal. America – land of the free – home of the twitter. Oh, and if you send a twitter it is called a tweet. The logic? I'm not sure. Maybe I'll do some research and get back to you. Maybe I'll send you a tweet. Ha ha ha. Sometimes my sense of humor cracks me up. Not literally – you twit.

Chapter XXXI. – Smoke and Croak – Part II
Or: Drugs

Sometimes, when I have nothing else to say, I start conversations with, "Back when I was a drug addict…" It's quite the icebreaker really. People seem to stop and pay attention.

The drug was nicotine, a drug so powerful that one Surgeon General of the United States called it more powerful than heroin. By the way, what kind of title is Surgeon General? While serving in that position, he or she neither operates on anyone nor leads any military forces. Brilliant. In fact, the Surgeon General's cousin, the Postmaster General doesn't see much combat either. Nor does the Attorney General. In fact, generally speaking, the entire General family seems misnamed. Maybe they should work for General Motors – or General Foods.

But back to the drug addiction. Most smokers don't admit to being drug addicts. They are. I know. Wake up and light a cigarette. Smoke with the morning coffee – when you start the car – when you talk on the phone – during 18 smoke breaks at work – and any other opportunity that occurs. Wake up in the middle of the night? Better light up. First cigarette is finished – still time left on the break? Chain smoke – light a second one with the remains of the first. Chain smoking. Smoking a chain. Sounds…dangerous. I teach students whose parents say they can't afford college. Mom and dad both smoke two packs a day – a $5,000 a year habit. Hmm…

I haven't smoked for over 20 years. But there was a time when I spent large sums of money to buy a product that shortened my life and made my breath stink. And my clothes stink. And the house stink. And my wife married me anyway. I must have been irresistible. And there's more. If you smoke, eventually you will participate in the dry lip finger slide and burn ritual. What happens is you take a drag of your cigarette. It is called a drag because... smoking is a drag? Cigarette companies sponsor drag racing? Drag queens are smokers? I don't know, but you take a drag and you think you are moving the cigarette from your mouth, only your lips are dry and the cigarette sticks to your lip, and your fingers slide down the length of the cancer stick, burning your index and middle finger, causing you to use most of the words George Carlin indentified as being unfit for television.

This may or may not cause hot coals to drop onto your lap, but even if this doesn't, eventually you will burn clothes, chairs, coaches, the rug, and who knows what else. It is especially fun to burn your pants while driving on the interstate.

75% of the United States does not smoke – at least that is what the newsman said recently. The other 25 % lives in Tennessee – or at least the tobacco belt. People in that belt also dip – or chew – or use smokeless tobacco. Even I was never that addicted. They put something in their mouths that, depending on the type of product, looks either like a handful of worms or coffee grounds. Some have a neat little pouch that contains the worms, or the coffee grounds, or ground-up worms, or whatever it is.

I really don't care so much about what people put in their mouths, after all, it's their mouth. I do care about what comes out. Few things are as gross or disgusting as tobacco juice – ambeer – that river of brown saliva that tobacco chewers share with the world. I've seen worm eaters expectorate (note the fancy word) enough fluid to float a small yacht. Wait – is there such a thing as a small yacht? Isn't that an oxymoron? And who in the name of Gilligan's Island decided to spell yacht with a "c" and an "h"?

I could go on and on about smoking. Fortunately, I won't. I just hope Sheryl doesn't smoke – or dip. And I think the leader of the United Nations – the Secretary General of the U.N. – should look into this. The Secretary General is another one of those weird general things. You know he doesn't file documents or answer phones or keep track of appointments. And he surely doesn't lead military maneuvers. I wonder if he goes around spitting tobacco juice into a Coke™ can. And I won't even mention the dumb pluralization (i.e. Surgeons General). Wait, I did mention it. I am sorry. Please don't call the Attorney General. He might call out the troops and attack me.

Chapter XXXII. – Awards
Or: Pushing the Envelope

I think we need more award shows. Stop screaming. I know we've got Tonys and Oscars and Obies and Emmys and Grammys and People's Choices and CMAs and Screen Actors and Cleos and Kennedy Center and others I'm too lazy to think about. But there are weekends (plural) where no one is getting recognized for anything. America – we can do better.

I did not mention Pulitzer and Noble prizes/awards because I didn't think of them in the first paragraph. I did in this paragraph, and I hope I win one soon – maybe for this book, especially after I help my fellow countrymen receive some recognition.

I say let's start with The Twitters. Or the Tweets. This would be great because there would be no acceptance speeches – just some flying fingers creating thank you images on the screen.

Remember *Rowan and Martin's Laugh-In*? You don't? Are you sure you are old enough to read this book? Anyway, the hosts – surprisingly named Rowan and Martin – used to give the Flying Fickle Finger of Fate award every week to someone who had done something incredibly stupid. Political figures dominated the award. I say bring it back. Actually, I'd like the entire show to be brought back. They could just rerun the show and when they got to the Flying Fickle Finger of Fate award, they could magically edit it so that a modern screw-up could be awarded the finger. Or The Finger.

The sports world is every bit as obsessed with awards as the rest of the country – most rebounds at night – most base hits on a Sunday – most touchdowns in games that start after 4:00. What if Congress adopted this model? Actually, if Congress adopted the model, there would be a scandal. But wouldn't it be fun to have to have a daily/weekly/monthly/yearly award show for our elected officials? Since "pork" has become a big issue, we could give an MVP (most valued porker) award to the person producing the most gratuitous spending for his/her district or state. The trophy could be shaped like a troth. We could give the Wilbur Mills award for the person caught in the most compromising position. The award would be shaped like a tidal basin. We could pass out a Bushy to the person who did the most damage to the English language, and a Clinton to the person who...well...acted the most like Clinton. That award would most likely be cigar-shaped.

Other awards I'd like to see:

- The Michael Vick Award to the person who throws away the most promising career.
- The Anita Bryant Tolerance Award to the person who makes the most hateful comments. Talk radio would own this one.
- The *Baywatch* Award given annually to the show with the highest ratings for no reason other than cleavage/bouncing bosoms/skimpy bathing suits. (Not that there's anything wrong with those things).

I'd like to suggest The Sheryl. It would go to the female singer who exemplifies the attributes of my best friend – brains, beauty, and charisma. She would have to write her own songs, and it would help is she had her own diddly squat. One star without squat is plenty. Oh, and another thing, let's identify the baseball player with the biggest chaw of tobacco and give him the Dumbass Award in the shape of... well...a dumbass (not to be confused with an intelligent ass).

And finally, let's give the Enron Award to every C.E.O. who runs his or her company into bankruptcy while collecting a huge salary/bonus/buy-out. And let's have a contest to design this award. Then we can have another award show to honor the winning designer.

Chapter XXXIII. – Words, Words, Words
Or: Bastards Among Us

I teach many teen-agers who babysit. They are babysitters. Ask them what they're doing this weekend, they'll say, "Babysittin' my nephew."

"How old is your nephew?"

"He's ten."

Ah, language. Baby sitting. Sitting on babies. Sounds…Criminal. If the teen-ager said, "I'm baby tending," or "Baby caring," or even, "Baby watching," people would look at said teen-ager with disdain, or datstain, or some stain, even though said teen-ager would be far more accurate. Why the phrase "said teen-ager" is used is also incomprehensible, but I can only deal with one idiocy at a time. I teach babysitters. That makes me sad. And they are proud of it. And it doesn't bother them that the so-called baby they are sitting is actually a ten-year old. And I may try to see how many sentences I can start with the word "and." And I don't care how many Curmudgeon Virgins go into convulsions.

So teen-agers are sitting on ten-year-old babies and the record for consecutive sentences that start with "and" is four. And I'm going to start another topic: Civil War. Say it with me, "Civil War." Kind, friendly, polite war. Don't call it uncivil war, that would be… well…correct. Can't have that. Just like we can't have a coldwater heater or the fair lines on a baseball field. Or a fair poll. Must be a foul poll – even if it is in fair territory. Because we said so – because it's always been that way -- because…well…dang it, it's our tradition and our heritage and that's that.

Which of course brings me to bastards. I'm not talking about the kind who cut you off when you're driving or talking. I'm talking about the archaic use, because a few days ago I heard a man refer to a kid as a "bastard child." He seemed to actually like the kid. He wasn't mad. He just matter-of-factly talked about the bastard child.

What did I do? Nothing, I am embarrassed to say. It took me a moment to process what I had heard, and I was, well…I guess I choked. Maybe it's not my place to go around "correcting" people. But I walked away incredulously.

First of all – who uses this phrase? I swear I hadn't heard it in decades. Secondly…WHY? A child, who has no control over the actions of his parents, is conceived out of wedlock, and bang – you, kid, are a bastard. Take that. That'll teach ya. Next time pick better sperm and egg donors – ya bastard. What is the opposite of, "Out of wedlock?" It should be, "in of wedlock." Of course it isn't. Somehow, it's just, "in wedlock." So…how many in wedlock babies have grown up to be real bastards? How many out of wedlock babies have grown up to be wonderful human beings?

Here's a scenario. Joe Dildo cheats on his wife and his taxes. Of course, he hasn't been caught yet, so everyone thinks he's a good guy. He rips off his company, is rude to waitresses, and loves child porn. He's a bastard by any definition, but no one calls him one. When Mrs. Dildo gives birth to their "in of wedlock" child, little Joe Dildo, Jr., he (Joe, Jr.) is greeted as a wonderful bundle of joy – the boy who will perpetuate the Dildo name and legacy. Meanwhile, Mr. Dildo's secretary is also pregnant. Guess who the father is? And guess who gets labeled the bastard when he's born?

Of course, there is another word some people love to use for these out of wedlock babies: Illegitimate. Much nicer than bastard. Look Ethel – it's the illegitimate child of Mr. Dildo's secretary. Aren't we kind – we didn't call him a bastard.

Who are the people who decide if another human being is legitimate or not? If you're not legit, do you still have to pay taxes? If a bastard child dies in the service of his country, does he become an unbastard? What percent of those who claim to be pro-life – who would castigate anyone who had an abortion – call the unaborted child an illegitimate bastard? I'm placing the number at 86.3%.

So there you have it. Teen-agers are sitting on ten-year-old baby bastards while their daddies are off fighting in civil wars. Some will be killed by friendly fire – which I guess is supposed to make their loved ones feel better.

Funeral Director: I am so sorry for your loss.

Distraught Widow: Thank you. But at least it was friendly fire during a civil war. I don't know what I would have done if he were killed by unfriendly fire in an uncivil war.

I'm glad that's over. I don't like to talk about things like that. Maybe the next chapter will be about sons of bitches. Never daughters of bitches, only sons. Or the quadratic formula. It's hard to beat the old q.f. for fun and pleasure. Yup – I just used the words quadratic formula, fun, and pleasure in the same sentence. I am amazingly talented. Take that, ya bastards.

Chapter XXXIV. – Facebook
Or: What am I doing?

I am on Facebook, although not literally. I will repeat that. I – a 57-year-old geezer, have joined the ranks of the Facebook fanatics.

Why am I on Facebook? I do not know. As a general rule, I dislike computers. Oh, they're fine when everything is working. But when they aren't functioning, they piss me off as much as a UT loss to Florida. Okay, maybe not quite that much, but you get the idea.

So the fact that I am on something that increases my computer contact time (or CCT) amazes me. I am obviously easily amazed.

One day I was cruising through life, oblivious to MySpace and Facebook and all the opportunities that exist to embarrass oneself in cyberspace. The next day – BAM – Facebook aliens abducted me and plastered all kinds of information about me all over the network. Actually, a friend convinced me to join, and I believe I was sober at the time. He said it was fun, and might be good for book sales, and really easy to do. He was right about that last part – I got my daughter to set up the entire thing. She explained what she was doing while I nodded and hoped she didn't see the glazed look in my eye. Okay, both eyes. Doesn't the word glazed make you think of donuts? What if you had a glazed look in one eye and a sprinkled look in the other? I am not going to write about that anymore because I'm starting to drool. Not on your page, silly reader. Just the original manuscript. If I were more creative and clever, or a more dedicated writer, I could create something that looked like drool on this page, but I can't be bothered. I have to check my Facebook pages.

Facebook is written as one word. We in the literary world call it a compound word. But the abbreviation for Facebook is always written FB. Since it is already international, I think it should be abbreviated FBI – but I don't think that will happen.

I like posting what's on my mind – on those rare occasions when something is actually on my mind. Most of the time I look at that inviting prompt, think, "I'm a writer, I can do this," then I stop. What if I write something weak, lame, or boring? Won't that reflect on my ability? What if I leave it blank? Won't people think less of me? What kind of writer can't write a simple sentence or two?

I enjoy reading all of the other posts. Okay – that's not accurate. I enjoy reading most of the other posts. Some are down-right hysterical. Some are upright hysterical, but I enjoy the down-rights better.

There are some – and I cringe to say this because they are "approved friends," not to be confused with disapproved friends, but…well…some people are just plain post happy. Some are fancy post happy, some are plain post sad, but the post happy people are annoying. They put out an update – a news bulletin on EVERY activity. Ray is trimming his nails now. Ray is braiding his ear hair now. Ray is posting a message now. Actually, that last one is mildly amusing – I might post that one tonight.

Then there are all of those tests. Take this test to see which *Star Wars* character you are. Take this one to see which state you should live in. Why? If I live in Tennessee and the test determines that I should live in Idaho, am I going to move? Take this test to see which movie most represents your life. That's a real recipe for disappointment. Can't you picture some poor, unbalanced slob who thinks his life is best reflected in *An Officer and a Gentleman* and the results say *Godzilla* or *Silence of the Lambs*? Might just push the poor boy over the edge.

There are thousands of tests being taken by thousands of people who couldn't wait to get out of school so they wouldn't have to take any more tests.

Of course, the real test is when you ask to be someone's friend. They get to confirm or ignore your request. You never actually get a rejection letter or anything, but if you haven't heard in six or seven months, you have a pretty good idea that you are a reject. I think the requested friend should have to send a response. The choices should be:

A) Yes, I'd love to confirm you as a friend
B) I am willing to confirm you on a trial basis, but don't send me any tests
C) Thanks, but no thanks
D) Are you kidding?

I also think the rejected party should be able to send a fist with a very large extended middle finger to the rejecter, but that's just me.

I'm still a Facebook novice (an FN – or an FBN) but there sure seems to be a lot of tagging going on. Someone is always being tagged in a photo or something. I'm not sure if it's freeze tag, where you have to stay still in cyberspace until someone unfreezes you, or if it's just regular tag where you are now it and have to tag someone else. Just what I wanted – a trip back to pre-puberty games. Yippee.

Some people have thousands of friends. I think they are inventing people and creating fake profiles. It's like a competition to see who can have the most friends – just like being in high school.

Of course, the more friends you have, the more postings you get to read. Some people need secretaries just to keep up with the incoming mail. Oh well.

Ray is having quality CCT on FB even if he is an FN, and he just finished the Which One of the Seven Dwarfs Would You Be Test. It came out Grumpy – because of the stupid test. LOL

Chapter XXXV. – Flyin' High
Or: Up, Up, and Away

I flew (in a plane) from Knoxville to Hartford, Connecticut recently. Of course, no one flies directly from Knoxville to Hartford. There is always, as in each and every time, the joyously named connecting flight. I actually had three choices of connecting flight locations this time.

Choice number one was Atlanta, also known as the fly south to go north choice. Choice two was Chicago – also known as the what in the hell, fly anywhere, who cares about logic choice. Choice number three was dumpy and dull Dulles, in our Nation's Capitol. I thought for three seconds and chose Dulles.

Of course, both sites of origin – isn't that a cute term – experienced delays, making the connecting experience a lot like an endurance contest/ sprint/ human obstacle course.

That is not the worst thing about flying.

Airlines have now gotten bizarre when it comes to luggage. First, there is the fifty pound rule. Fliers are now faced with a fine if any suitcase weighs more than fifty pounds. For longer vacations, that is a difficult task, especially since some empty suitcases weigh twenty pounds. Of course, a person with two fifty pound bags is okay, but a person with one fifty-one pounder is in trouble. Fines will be imposed.

I was going on a short trip. I only had thirty-five pounds of luggage, but my airline charged me $15 just for handling the bag. Both ways. I don't want to identify these thieves, I mean this service provider, but I didn't fly divided, and their skies would have been a whole lot friendlier without the extra $30.00. This is not the worst thing about flying.

Once upon a time, vehicles did not have seatbelts. This was B.S. (before seatbelts – or maybe it was B.S.B., but who really cares?). When the seat belt because a standard feature on cars and planes, some people needed instruction on this unique, unfamiliar device. Those days are long gone, but airlines insist on demonstrating how to fasten this complicated apparatus, even though three-year-olds can do it. I always feel sorry for those flight attendants, who offer all kinds of info. that absolutely no one listens to. It's a lot like teaching. But this is not the worst thing about flying – nor is the so-called food (if it is even served at all) nor the cramped space nor the air turbulence nor the suspense as you wait at the baggage claim. The absolute worst thing about flying is O.P. – other people – also known as dickweeds in flight.

If I ever take a flight free of:

A) The woman who bathed in perfume

B) Crying babies

C) Coughing, hacking passengers

D) Loud, rude, pushy jerks

I just might dance in the aisle with the flight attendant and hold the seatbelt for her as she demonstrates its intricacies. Not that there is any danger. There is one antidote to most of the O.P. craziness. I used to think that the iPod™ was invented for people suffering with crying babies. I now know there are other important uses.

By the way, why is it called an iPod™ if it goes in your ears? Okay, I know the actual iPod™ doesn't go in your ear – only the headphones do. And yes, I know it is not spelled e-y-e. But still – you listen to it. I think it should be called an earPod (no ™ necessary). And you use headphones – even though they cover or fit into what? Say it with me...the ears. But if you say that you were listening to music from your earPod through your earphones, you are the crazy one.

On my flight from Dulles to Connecticut, I sat in the middle seat. King Kong was on my left and Godzilla was on my right. Except Godzilla was suffering from allergies, or the plague, and he sniffed constantly, pausing occasionally to wheeze and sneeze and cough and snort. It got so bad I put my earphones on, even though they were not connected to my earPod. It seems that earPods can cause jets to crash if you use them at unauthorized times – so I wasn't about to bring down the plane. The earphones helped, but I still heard Mr. Sniffleupagus so I started timing his snorts. He averaged six sniffs a minute – one every ten seconds. Fortunately, we reached a point where I could turn on my earPod, and the friendly skies were sniff free.

Which brings me to Pluto – or the planet formerly known as Pluto – or the former planet known as Pluto. I'm not implying that I went to Pluto – I was very content making it to Connecticut. But something made me think Pluto – I believe it was the earPod.

For most of my life, Pluto was the smallest and most distant planet in our solar system. Then, one day, through no fault of its own, BAM! Pluto is out of the solar system pool – banished to non-planet status. I'm not trying to live in the past. I'm not opposed to scientific advancements. I've read the reasoning behind the declassification. I even understood some of it. But it does shake one's confidence. What scientific truths do I accept today that will be disproved tomorrow? I mean, if Pluto can go for a century or so and be a planet – then it's not – what's next? Will Disney throw out the dog of the same name? It boggles the mind.

Which brings me to Uranus. As of this moment, Uranus is still a planet. Only its name has been changed – or at least the pronunciation has. There was a time when this planet was pronounced Yur – anus – accent on the second syllable. For junior high boys, it caused uncontrollable fits of laughter. It quickly became everyone's favorite celestial body – at least until we discovered *Playboy*. Even trusted, patriotic Americans pronounced it Yur anus. I'm almost positive Walter Cronkite said it that way. Then, suddenly, somehow, word got out – a declaration was...well...declared, and immediately people started saying, Yur ah ness – accent on the first syllable. I strongly suspect the Curmudgeon Virgins were behind this, but I cannot prove it. All I know is Pluto is gone and junior high kids no longer get to talk about yur anus and life is just not the same.

And my earPod takes care of crying babies and giants with the sniffles, but we need something to combat the women who bathe in perfume and the men who swim in aftershave. Can you say nosePod?

Chapter XXXVI. – American Idle
Or: Idol Minds

American Idol is the number one show in the country. What does that say about us? I watch it. What does that say about me?

I am embarrassed to admit that I watch that stupid show. I think substantially less of myself for doing so – but I do. Two nights a week. Yuck.

American Idol represents everything I hate about the music industry. It is pre-packaged, style and sex appeal over substance, manufactured pop star pabulum. And I tune in without fail. I am a moron.

American Idol has done one positive thing for me. There was a time when I thought I might be the worst singer in the world. I now know that I am not even the worst singer in the U.S. I still suck – but there are worse. And, whereas I know I suck, they apparently think they are good. So I am also smarter than they are. Even though I am a moron, I did not spend time and money travelling to audition. I did not wait for days in long lines only to humiliate myself on national T.V.

I wonder how many contestants are the result of drunken fraternity/ sorority bets or dares. I hope a lot – at least they have an excuse.

I wonder if FOX pays some people to act like idiots. I hope so. The early auditions are mildly amusing. Terrible singers cuss out judges for not appreciating their "talents." Clueless contestants prance about in costumes from Mardi Gras or a gay pride parade. It's all good.

Then the contest gets "serious." By serious I mean filled with commercials. I believe a two hour A.I. show has twenty-five minutes of singing, ten minutes of judges' comments, and eighty-five minutes of commercials. This is why the DVR was invented – so a person can watch a two hour show in thirty-five minutes. That's if you care what the judges say.

I totally care about what the judges say. Actually, I only partially care, but no one ever says that. Except me. Starting now. I want to see how many times Randy uses the words dog and pitchy. I want to see Simon (a.k.a Mr. Nasty) be his warm and pleasant self. I want to mine for logic in the fertile fields of Paula's mind (and to see if she's sober). I want to see Kara…well actually, I just want to see Kara – who cares what she says.

Then there is the "results show." American has voted. One person will be eliminated. This takes an hour.

This past week the theme was "disco music." I'll ignore the obvious cheap line about disco music being an oxymoron. I'll ignore my reaction when I learned that disco music was the theme, because writing about a moron screaming, "No" and "Why?" and "Are you kidding me?" is just not how I want people to picture me. Instead, I'll go directly to the results show, where three out of shape icons of the disco era (also known as "IDES") reprised their hits that they can no longer perform. It was riveting entertainment. Someone should have warned us to beware the IDES of April.

Then, the most annoyingly saccharine contestant from last year's contest came out to add to the fun. By then, several of this year's contestants volunteered to be eliminated so they could escape the torture, but plucky Ryan "I Have the Best Job on T.V. and I'm Better Than You" Seacrest intervened and restored order and sent someone home.

Next week there will be five finalists. The theme will be "songs you sang in second grade." I'm looking forward to *The Itsy Bitsy Spider* and *I'm a Little Teacup*. The result show will feature Shirley Temple's greatest hits and clips of *Romper Room*.

A few paragraphs ago, I abbreviated *American Idol*. I called it A.I. There was also a movie called A.I. In that case it stood for Artificial Intelligence. Coincidence? I think not.

Can you imagine the legends of years gone by competing on this show? Keep in mind, original songs are not allowed. Can't be having song writers compete. They're only the backbone of the music industry. My mind pictures Bob Dylan and Neil Young and Bob Marley and the individual members of the Beatles trying to perform in this format. (Individual Beatles because there are absolutely, positively, no groups allowed). What a fiasco that would have been.

I wonder if there is any member of the rock and roll hall of fame who could have survived this show. I doubt it. Picture Eric Clapton doing movie or Broadway tunes, or Janis Joplin doing disco, or Jimi Hendrix doing 50's music. Yuck.

Yet it remains the top rated show each week – and even people who get eliminated make millions of dollars. Meanwhile, on street corners and in pubs and cafés all over America, there are talented people struggling to eat while they sing and play their instruments and write their hearts out.

I'm sure glad my true hero – the real idol of America, my dear friend Sheryl didn't have to go on a show like that. It would have cost me a fortune to keep voting for her. That's right – America gets to call or text, but there is a cost for doing so. The phone companies love this show. Coca-Cola™ likes this show – since the judges are required to have these huge red glasses with the word Coke™ printed on them. Somehow, Ford™ got involved – the "idols" make commercials for and ride around in this company's vehicle.

Oh well. If you can't beat 'em – join in.

They're all little teapots
Short and stout
Randy says it's cool
The way you worked it out.

Simon laughed at Paula
So she just pouts
And Ryan asked Kara
If she wants to go out.

It was a little pitchy, but I worked it out.

Chapter XXXVII. – Unbelievable Or: What?

There are some things I have trouble believing. Maybe that's not exactly right. I guess I CAN believe them, I just don't want to. For example, why does America, land of the, "We're number one" chant, require everything to be filled out using a number two pencil? It seems un-American to me. We should have red, white, and blue pencils – number one pencils – and nothing else. Let's sell those number two pencils to the rest of the inferior world.

As I write this, there is a swine flu epidemic, or a pandemic, or a superdemic, or whatever the latest term is. It's been on the news for the last 12,978 hours. So here's a pop quiz for Americans: What is a swine? I'll give a mom quiz later – for now it's just a pop quiz. Numerous people of the teen-ager persuasion, my students to be specific, many with passionate opinions about this issue, have proven to be unaware of the definition of the word swine. Sometimes the words "passionate opinions" are euphemisms for "uninformed ranting."

I wonder how many of my teen-agers' parents would fail this pop quiz. Or this mom quiz: Since you have strong opinion about the war in Iraq, go to the map and point to that country. We've only been fighting there since 2003. If you can't do it, you must forfeit the right to use political bumper stickers.

Here are some other almost unbelievable things:

- Donald Trump still has a T.V. show.
- States in the Bible belt lead the nation in teen-age pregnancy. Way to go Bible-belters.
- Professional wrestling and roller derby still exist.
- The Cubs still have huge crowds after a century of disappointments.
- People still call certain types of unrealistic T.V. programs "reality shows."
- Billy Mayes sells more products now than ever – even after those earlier products have proven to be worthless.
- Teen-agers are the only group in America that continues to show an increase in the use of tobacco products. Way to go teen-agers.
- Educators still give standardized tests, even though we know they are crap. Way to go educators.
- Politicians continue to lie and cheat and cover-up – even though it is ALWAYS the lie and the cover-up that cause the biggest problem. Way to go politicians.
- Athletes and celebrities continue to beat up people – including their so-called loved ones. Way to go athletes and celebrities.

For those who failed the pop quiz a swine is a pig. Not the human kind of pig – the kind who run Ponzi Schemes and companies like Enron and certain banks. No – not that kind of pig. A swine is a four-legged barnyard animal that squeals, or oinks, or grunts while wallowing in the mud. Okay, I know some women who do that also, but they don't have four legs.

If you failed the mom quiz – the one about locating Iraq on a map, well…If this were a classier publication, it would include a map on this page. There would be a place for the reader to place an "X" on his or her state, with the words, "You are here" above the United States. Then a dotted line would lead from the east coast of the U.S. to the country of Iraq.

I am truly sorry this is not a classier publication. It would have been so educational – and colorful. You know what else could and should be educational and colorful? Schools. I believe that will happen about the same time a map magically appears on this page. But that is another issue for another book.

Currently, I'm more interested in cleavage. Actually, that is a misleading sentence. It might lead some of my gentle readers, even my especially astute ones, to believe that my cleavage interest (or C.I.) is new – or only a current fad. That would be wrong, wrong, wrong, oh so wrong gentle readers.

I have been interested in and appreciative of cleavage since… since…since the Johnson administration…since I learned to say the word "hooter"…since I saw my first glossy centerfold. (I am sure it is only a coincidence that it was during the Johnson administration).

In fact, since my C.I. is also an appreciation as well as an interest, I will declare myself a member of the C.I.A. I will avoid all of the undercover jokes.

The subject of cleavage arose because:

A) I was tired of the other topics
B) It's a fun topic
C) It's a fun word to say
D) There seems to be a lot of it on display these days.

I know, there are those in our society who are appalled by this display of the female anatomy. They would prefer much more modestly dressed women. To those quasi-Curmudgeon Virgin types, I say, "Stop being such killjoys."

Cleavage watching is good, cheap, wholesome entertainment. It is safer than NASCAR and healthier than junk food. And, since it clearly is unavoidable, I say viva la boobie. I'm not sure when cleavage started busting out all over the place, or why. It just seems that everywhere I turn – Whoop – there it is (to quote an old and terrible song).

It is almost unbelievable, but unlike all of the other unbelievable stuff, this is something that makes life more pleasant.

That's all I want to say about cleavage – even though I'm writing – not talking. I would be interested in what you find to be hard to believe or accept. Not so interested that I'll give you my email address, but interested. In the meantime – or in the not so mean time – in the pleasant time – I've got work to do. The C.I.A. is a full time commitment.

Chapter XXXVIII. – Sequels
Or: Variations on a Theme

If a book or movie has success, there will be sequels or copycats or more of the same. I'm surprise some haven't been written for the classics.

Book and/or movie titles I would like to see:
- *A Grape in the Sun*
- *The Raisins of Wrath*
- *The Sun Also Sets*
- *A Streetcar Named Denial*
- *A Pitcher in the Rye*
- *A Catcher in the Wheat*
- *To Kill a Blue Jay*
- *To Coddle a Mockingbird*
- *The Young Man and the Sea*
- *The Old Man and the Viagra*
- *Lord of the Fleas*
- *The Mediocre Gatsby*
- *The Chartreuse Letter*
- *Desert Gump*
- *Low Noon*
- *Dog on a Cold Tin Roof*
- *The Even Couple*
- *Butterflies are Expensive*

- *Supper at Tiffany's*
- *Breakfast at Hardee's*™
- *East Side Story*
- *Blueberry Finn*
- *A Massachusetts Yankee in King Arthur's Court*
- *A Thanksgiving Carol*
- *The Grinch that Stole Easter*

Wow. I could do this all day. I think I will. No – wait – I have C.I.A. work to attend to, but when I'm done... And I haven't even done song titles, like *Escalator to Heaven* or *Blue-Eyed Girl* or *Come Tuesday* or *Hotel Arizona* or... Well... I just may have to do another chapter on this. I wonder what kind of breath you will be waiting with. Not baited breath. Please – not that. May your breath always be unbaited.

Chapter XXXIX. – Bone Pickin' Or: Packaging

I have a bone to pick with our society. Not literally of course – that would be disgusting. How do these phrases worm their way into our speech? Why do I still use them? Isn't worming an awesome word? I'll bet the cavemen had something to do with it. No offense Geico™ Neanderthals.

My complaint for the moment is the crap one has to go through to get to the new product one has spent his or her hard earned money to purchase. Even if it was easy earned money, the packaging on new products is a national problem that needs to be addressed just as soon as we have a college football playoff. BTW (that's electronic communication shorthand for by the way for you Neanderthals of the Geico™ and non-Geico™ variety) -- Congress has held hearings about the issue of an NCAA football play-off. That's right – Congress.

I may have mentioned a time or six that I am in favor of a playoff. Just in case – I really, really, really want a playoff. BUT – I really, really, really want Congress to BUTT OUT! If there is one thing college football does not need it is interference from some politically motivated, money hungry, vote grubbing geezers on Capitol Hill.

But back to the issue a hand – or at foot – since we were taking football. I buy a shirt. I bring shirt home. I cut plastic "tees" that have been randomly stuck through 22 different places of my shirt. This cannot be good for the fabric. I have to cut the plastic tee and pull it out of the fabric while making sure the tee does not fall on the floor, because it immediately becomes invisible if it does. This is especially true if it falls into carpet – where it can hide for decades, only to emerge when someone is walking barefoot across the floor. How it manages to always land sharp point up is one of society's greatest mysteries.

Some shirts are neatly folded when you purchase them. To keep them neatly folded, pins are inserted. My personal record is 18 pins. 18 freakin' pins! One might think that that would equate to 18 pinholes – but one would be wrong. Double and triple penetration of folded fabric makes the number much greater.

I repeat – people are putting holes in my clothes – on purpose. And I am not pleased about this, and since other people buy clothes, I'm assuming they have plastic tees and/or pins in their stuff as well. It is time to stop quietly accepting this indignity. We must stop suffering in silence. We must demand that Congress stop interfering with football and start addressing this invasion of our clothing.

BTW, has anyone ever met a person who admitted to being the plastic tee inserter? I have not. Clearly someone, actually lots of someones, put the tees in the clothes. But I have never talked to a person who has done so. Maybe they are too embarrassed to admit it.

"Hey Johnny, what do you want to do when you grow up?"

"I want to shove plastic tees into people's clothes."

"Me too. Maybe we can go into business together."

And it doesn't end there. Some items have a twenty pound circular disc attached to a plastic base by means of a 12 inch cork screw. It takes a special tool to remove it. This is supposed to prevent shoplifting, or keep plastic widget cork screw doohickey manufacturers in business.

Our aspirin bottles are tougher to enter than Fort Knox. The final little barrier over the top of the bottle is made of some kind of foil that NEVER pulls off evenly.

CDs come in a bionic plastic wrap that requires a machete to open. Once that wrap is off, the real fun begins. To open the CD, one has to remove a seal that runs the length of the top – a sticker sealed with crazy glue on steroids.

Electronic equipment like computers or DVD players comes packaged in enough material to fill a landfill. Huge boxes – tons of Styrofoam™, yards of tape, and plastic wrap.

Of course, products are not the only things packaged in America. People are packaged as well, especially those running for political office. One of my heroes, Jackson Browne, once wrote, *"They sell us the president / The same way / They sell us our clothes and our cars."* And he wrote it more than two decades ago. He also wrote, *"They sell us everything from youth to religion / The same way they sell us our wars."*

Of course the sellers couldn't sell if we didn't buy it. When I say "we," I mean everyone in America except me and the other intellectuals who are reading this book.

Man – writing this chapter has worn me out. Too much stuff to think about. Let's review: With two wars waging, the economy in trouble, a swine flu epi, pan, or superdemic, and problems with the environment, education, and health care – Congress is talking about football while ignoring the destruction of America's clothing. Meanwhile, it takes an act of Congress to open most of our products. Scratch that. Not literally. That is the dumbest sentence in the entire book. I should get rid of it – an act of Congress would not help me reach my CD any quicker – in fact, it might slow me down.

I need to go back to writing about cleavage. No packaging problems there.

Chapter XL. – Cat Skinning
Or: Fish In the Sea

There is more than one way to skin a cat – but why in the hell would you want to? I've heard this phrase several times recently, and each time I wanted to ask the genius who used it, "Really? How many ways can you name? Have you personally tried them? Which one is your favorite?"

Actually, I did ask those questions, but the speaker was on television and apparently he could not hear me through the set.

More than one way to skin a cat – indeed. It's about as helpful as telling someone who is in agony over a break-up, "Don't worry – there are plenty of fish in the sea." I wonder how the person being told that really wants to respond to the well-intended but unhelpful phrase. A few suggestions:

- "Really? I didn't know that."
- "So what are you saying – we should go fishing?"
- "Thanks – that means a lot – I guess I'll just forget about the last five years I've wasted on someone who no longer loves me."
- "Yeah – I know – lots of fish – but I DATE PEOPLE you moron."
- "Good one. Why don't you go cuddle with a cod or flirt with a flounder or seduce a salmon."

I kinda like those alliterative, suggestive fish references. I was going to get crude (or gross) and use bang a bass or shag a shark (which sounds dangerous) or even pork a perch, but I chose not to. I am proud of that decision – and the one to avoid blowfish and humpbacks all together.

I didn't want to get on anyone's first nerve. I didn't want to put my worst foot forward. I just wanted to write the best thing since unsliced bread. My cup runneth under with pride. I didn't want the bare facts, I wanted the clothed ones. I didn't want the naked truth either – I wanted my truth to be just like my facts – free of any wardrobe malfunctions. It's not that I don't like nudity, it's just that some things are better covered – things like truth and facts and Donald Trump. It's plain as night.

Which brings me to space. Outer space. You know why? I will tell you. We just launched the space shuttle on a mission to fix the Hubble telescope. When I say "we" I mean NASA. I wasn't involved. This is considered a dangerous mission – so much so that a second shuttle – a rescue shuttle – is already on the launch pad ready to go. Why is this mission so dangerous? Litter. Space litter. *Parade Magazine* estimates that there are 17,000 pieces of space junk floating through space. Actually, floating isn't accurate – the junk is flying or hurtling or zooming through space at 20,000 miles per hour, and if our litter hits an astronaut or the shuttle or the Hubble – KaBoom!

So…Man has littered outer space! Just rolled down the shuttle window and pitched some leftover Tang™ out the opening. That's the first straw, as far as I'm concerned.

I realized some might find the jump from fish to outer space a strange one – but I mentioned Donald Trump, thought of his hair and…viola…space litter.

Which brings me to what I really wanted to write about in this chapter. I'd like to call it the essential questions of our time – questions like:

- Why do people continue to interview Darth Vader (a.k.a. Dick Cheney?)
- Why do we continue to have beauty pageants?

- Why do people who swear they need a break – a vacation – to get away from it all – take their cell phones and laptops and Blackberries™ with them?
- How many reunion tours can a rock band have before people stop going? (Actually, I believe the answer is twelve).
- Why do people who suck at parenting have so many kids?
- Who put the bop in the bop she bop she bop? (Yeah, I know it's an old question from an old song – but who did it? The same guy who let the dogs out?) I really want to know.

I believe that is just about enough essential questions for one chapter. I feel better now. I think I'll go grope a grouper.

Chapter XLI. – Animal Cruelty
Or: Classic Literature

So I'm writing this memorable, epic masterpiece called *In Search of Diddly Squat*, a work of art that you are currently reading and no doubt enjoying. You may be saying, "Hot damn – this just may be the most memorable, epic masterpiece I have ever read." If that is true, then:

A) You need to read more
B) You need to stop saying "Hot damn"
C) You need to buy more copies to give to everyone on your Christmas list.

One chapter of this memorable, epic masterpiece (or M.E.M.) began with these words:

"There is more than one way to skin a cat – but why in the hell would you want to?" Since I wrote those soon to be immortal words, I have twice heard someone say something almost as disgusting. People seem to get very excited about the opportunity to kill two birds with one stone. Again – why in the hell would you want to? I know the figurative meaning – but why does killing wildlife always rear its ugly head? And why do you rear a head? Shouldn't you rear a butt? And how do we know the head is ugly? So many questions – so few answers.

I just get sick (but not tired) of hearing about skinning cats and killing birds and horses of different colors – when clearly some horses have the same colors. I'm a little tired (but not sick) of busy beavers and busy bees. I'm sure there are lazy, unproductive beavers who sit on their butts while all the other beavers do the dam work – and I'm sure there are lazy-ass bees who just sit around the hive swilling honey and getting a buzz. Do we ever hear about them? We do not.

We do hear from the man (or woman) in the street. Constantly. This is more annoying than busy beavers. It happened this morning. Of course, when I say this morning, I mean the morning I was writing this M.E.M. By the time you read it, it will be a different morning. I'm sure you will understand.

This morning, the issue was the new environmental standards cars are going to be required to meet in the future. It went something like, "Car owner, meet the environmental standards." Maybe they shook hands or something. People from the administration, the auto industry, and the E.P.A. were interviewed. Political opponents were interviewed. Fair enough. Then, one random man in the street was questioned. As he was answering, his name appeared on the screen. Under his name was the word "Driver." That's it. That's all we know about this man in the street. He drives – and clearly that makes his opinion newsworthy.

He could have been a wanted axe murderer (although who would actually murder an axe?) He might be the world's worst driver. He might be on his way to have an affair with his best friend's wife. It doesn't matter. He talks into the microphone and somehow becomes the representative voice of authority and public opinion. WHY? And why is it always called the man in the street when he is clearly not in the street? In fact, in this case, he wasn't even on the street. He was on the sidewalk.

This happens far too often. Please, American T.V. news shows, Stop It! It's like they've run out of ways to present information. And when I watch the news, I'd like some facts. Not – "Hey, we need an opinion on the war in Iraq – let's ask this woman." The woman may be dumber than dirt – but we'll ask her. "Say, what about the deficit? Let's wake-up the local wino and see what he thinks."

Which brings me to the *Beverly Hillbillies,* or more specifically, the *Beverly Hillbillies'* theme song. Once a month, some clever person decides to take a political issue and write a song about it – and the words are always sung to the theme of the *Beverly Hillbillies.* It was funny and clever the first 87 times. Okay – maybe not than many. But it is no longer funny or clever. It is now lame and boring. So stop it.

No, seriously, no more
"Come and listen to a story
'Bout a man named Obama
Came ridin' into town
On some big and hairy llama."

I never actually heard that one, but there are plenty like it. I was going to rhyme Obama with your momma, but I didn't. And I still want to write his last name with an apostrophe. You know – O'bama – the Irish guy.

I just realized that I mentioned busy beavers and ignored their first cousins – the eager beavers. Sorry, eager beavers.

Let's review. No more hillbilly songs. No random man or woman in the street interviews. No more dumb animal references. Don't pull the wool over your eyes, because that is way too painful and kinky. Just clam up. Nothing fishy – no ox to gore. Let's just be like the month of March and go out like a lamb. A busy, eager lamb.

Cold damn – this is another great M.E.M. chapter.

Chapter XLII. – Up in Smoke
Or: Skunks and Fish

We interrupt this regularly scheduled chapter to bring you the following public service announcement. Actually, "we" is incorrect, since I am writing this all by myself. It's lonely work. But all public service announcements begin with the word we. I was just mindlessly following the accepted form. I apologize. Now – the P.S.A.

If you ride a bike on a path that you have to share with walkers and joggers and you ride up behind them and zoom past them without ringing a bell or otherwise announcing your presence, you are a BIG TIME DICKWEED. "We" now return to our regularly scheduled chapter.

Back when I was a drug addict…I enjoy beginning conversations with that little ice breaker – even in the summer when there is no ice left to break, and I may have used that once before in this book, but I don't care. I should begin, "Back when I was a legal drug addict…" because the drug was nicotine, a totally legal, destructive product. It has been twenty years since I've sucked in that poison, but here in the tobacco belt, there are many who still do. Suckers.

If a person smokes a lot, someone will inevitably say that he or she "smokes like a chimney." I guess that's fair – I mean chimneys certainly spew out lots of smoke. Except that in East Tennessee I use my fireplace about three months out of the year, so someone who smokes like my chimney doesn't smoke for three-fourths of the year.

Some people smoke so much they are called chain smokers. I've never actually tried to smoke a chain. I wouldn't even know how or where to light one, and they've got to be awkward to puff on, but they're probably no worse than cigarettes.

People who drink a lot are said to drink like a fish. Ha ha-ho ho-hee hee – What? "Drink like a fish?" I'm pretty sure fish don't drink. If they do, it's only water. So why did they become the animal representative of human over-indulgence? Once again, the animal kingdom is unfairly portrayed.

And it doesn't end with fish. Apparently, people are incapable of saying that someone has had too much to drink and letting it go with that. Even a simple, "He's drunk" doesn't work. We humans seem to need a comparison. We feel obligated to tell how drunk someone is, and how that compares to other drunken behavior. Hence the brilliant, "He's drunk as a skunk."

Drunk as a skunk? Raise your hand if you have ever seen a skunk even slightly tipsy. I'm sure there are three people out there in readership land who have:

A) Had a pet skunk and given it a beer, or
B) Had some berries in their yard that fell off the bush and fermented and were eaten by a skunk who then staggered around the yard harassing other skunks and engaging in other obnoxious skunky behavior, or
C) I actually can't think of a scenario for choice "C," and I can't believe someone would waste good beer on a pet skunk, so I'm going to start a new paragraph.

How did drunk as a skunk gain acceptance in our culture? Was there a committee? (It sounds like something a committee would create). Maybe there was a convention. A group of intellectuals convened to discuss which animal to use to denigrate human drunkenness, and since the skunk was unpopular anyway, it was decreed that, henceforth, forthwith, presto change-o – inebriated people are drunk as a skunk.

I believe the skunk barely beat out the aardvark. We would be saying "Drunk as an aardvark" except aardvark had too many syllables. It's harder to say – especially if one has been drinking.

Which reminds me of blimps. Not people who are too large – I'm talking about the things that float in the sky at every major sporting even in America.

I like blimps. I'd like to fly in one. Sometimes, blimps provide beautiful aerial pictures of football games, or even golf shots if one is desperate for a sporting event or in need of a sedative. Yup – blimps are pretty cool – most of the time.

But, like most things in America, someone will always find a way to screw up a good thing. In this case, it is the person who decided blimps should cover basketball games...or football games played in a dome.

Basketball games are played in a gym. Even if it is a large gym – so large it is called a coliseum, or even a garden, it is still a gym. Garden is a little weird – there are no fruits or vegetables or flowers – even in the square garden in New York. But a blimp flying over a gym gives the viewer at home a wonderful shot of...say it with me...a freakin' roof. "Oh look – it's the roof of the building where the game is being played. How exciting..."

It's even worse at night. You see lights. Street lights. Maybe the well-lit parking lot. That's it. I wonder how much it costs to send up a blimp so it can show us the top of a dome?

My favorite would be a hot, summer night, with a blimp sponsored by some life insurance company, showing us the roof of Syracuse University's Carrier™ Dome – a facility named for a heating and air conditioning company, perhaps the only major dome that does not have air conditioning. The GameDay crew would be there, saying:

Chris: Here's the view from the blimp.

Lee: It looks like a dome.

Kirk: That's right, Lee; it is a dome.

Lee: I knew it!

Chris: Now, back to the game.

Lee: It sure is hot in here.

This kind of talk is called – in technical circles – banter. Friendly banter. Even in technical squares and triangles – friendly banter. After three hours of friendly banter, you know what happens? Moe, Larry, and Curly go to a bar where they chain smoke like chimneys, drink like fish, and get drunk as aardvarks. And, since they are celebrities, they probably eat and drink for free. The richer you are, the more likely you are to get free food, because...well...just because. It's the American way.

I interrupt this chapter to bring you a public service announcement: If you ride a bike on a path that you have to share with walkers and joggers and you ride up behind them and zoom past them without ringing a bell or otherwise announcing your presence, you are a BIG TIME DICKWEED.

Some astute readers are probably saying, "Heavens to Betsy, Ray, that's the same P.S.A. you used to start this chapter. Have you lost your cotton-picking mind?"

First of all, astute readers, who in the hell is Betsy? And don't you think heavens to Betsy is a little strong?

Secondly, yes – I do realize I used the same P.S.A. twice. It's a technique we in the teaching profession call drill and review. It is a way of emphasizing the most important points. It is also a way of filling time when we've got nothing else to say, but I digress.

Thirdly, astute readers, neither my mind nor any other body part has recently picked any cotton. For the purposes of this chapter, recently is defined as any time during the first fifty-seven years of my life.

Finally, and sadly, yes dear readers, I think I have lost my mind. I am not sure how, or where, or when, but I do seem to have misplaced it. I miss it. But, I do take comfort in the realization that clearly I am not alone.

Chapter XLIII. – Doodlin'
Or: Macaroni

Remember Yankee Doodle? How about his younger brothers, Howdie Doodle and Cocka Doodle? Or his long-lost cousin, the rapper Snoopa Doodle? Okay, I may have made those up, but all patriotic Americans know about Yankee Doodle.

For the unpatriotic Americans, Yankee Doodle rode his pony into town one day. There, he performed one of the grandest feats ever immortalized in song. He stuck a feather in his hat. Yes he did – right there in front of – as they say in the South – God 'n everybody. And once the feather was securely stuck in his hat, he labeled it, "Macaroni." I am now going to skip a few lines to allow my readers to contemplate the ramifications of this act.

Are you done contemplating? Have you reached the only logical conclusion? I'm sure you have. That's right gentle readers – Yankee Doodle was stoned.

How else do you explain this totally bizarre behavior? Ole Yankee didn't know his ass from his elbow macaroni.

I am surprised this epic song hasn't spawned a major motion picture. Maybe songs are incapable of spawning – but if they could, the movie would appear thusly:

Wide angle shot of unsteady rider on a horse – like a male Lady Godiva only fully clothed – which is to say nothing like her at all, except he is riding side-saddle.

The horse stops and the camera pans to a feather that is floating, hovering, and flitting in the air – just like the one in *Forrest Gump*. The feather approaches Yankee, who tries to capture it but only succeeds in falling off his horse.

Camera pans to snickering crowd, then back to Doodle, who giggles as he tried to mount his trusty steed. It is notable that all steeds are always trustworthy, while so few of their riders are. Actually, Doodle didn't try to mount his steed, he just tried to get back in the saddle, which he eventually does. For reasons defying logic and gravity, the feather is still there. This time, Yankee Doodle plucked it from the air, stuck it in his hat, and said, "Whoa...like wow...Macaroni."

Camera pans back to show the crowd cheering and exchanging high fives and passing around various and sundry "peace pipes."

What a song! They just don't make 'em like that anymore (say hallelujah). Or like the one that made millions for Perry Como. Sing it with me – *"Hot diggity, dog diggity, boom what you do to me/ It's so new to me/ What you do to me."*

Hot diggity? I'll bet ole Perry was hell with the women. Just like Dean Martin when he sang about a moon in the sky hittin' your eye like a big pizza pie. Yup – that's amore all right.

I guess the key to a successful song is to mention food – be it macaroni (but no cheese), or hot diggity dogs, or pizza.

Of course Madison Avenue has known this for years. That's why members of my generation know all about bologna that has a first name. I can spell it for you – not that I will. And even though many of us have trouble remembering the names of our children, we can immediately recognize the product that consists of two all beef patties, special sauce, lettuce, cheese, pickles, onions on a sesame seed bun. That is not to suggest I can't remember my kids' names, because I can. Of course, I only have two. Some people have it much harder than I do. George Foreman found a solution to that – he named all of his kids George. Boys, girls, it didn't matter.

I'm not bitter, but some advertising person made bookoos of money by having a certain round white tablet with skinny arms and legs run around singing, "Plop, plop, fizz, fizz, oh what a relief it is." It's hard to beat lyrics like that – although we should try, with a baseball bat. That person later became a lyricist for Perry Como. A bookoo of money is larger than a truckload but smaller than the sum a fired SEC coach gets. I still think Yankee Doodle is the best. I was going to say Yankee Doodle takes the cake, but I didn't. In fact, I'm sure he did take the cake. You know he had a serious case of the munchies.

Chapter XLIV. – The Cherub
Or: Piss Me Off

A man sits down with a sketch pad. He creates a cartoon-like character – a caricature of a little boy with a small body, a large head, and a sardonic smile – like Dennis the Menace with an attitude – or a drug problem. This "cherub's" sole purpose in life is to pee on things.

You know the character I am talking about. He adorns numerous vehicles – especially pick-up trucks. Sometimes he wears the New York Yankees logo and pees on the logo of the Red Sox. Sometimes he wears a Sox logo and aims his stream at the Yankees. NASCAR fans love the little pisser, having him wear the number of their favorite driver while taking a leak on the number of their least favorite driver. Or maybe he is leaving a leak. I do not know who created this...this urination specialist. I know I said that it was a man. I know it could conceivably be a woman – but what are the odds? I suppose I could try to Google™ this – but what would I type in? Boy who pees? Besides, I don't really care who did it – I'd forget his name in five minutes anyway. I would like to know why he did it, and if he had any idea he would make so much money.

What I really want to do is talk to the people who adorn their vehicles with this classy kid. "Hey – do you know you've got a urinator on your back window?" I can't think of a better conversation starter. I can only imagine where it would go from there. I'm not going to write about it – only imagine it. You can join me if you wish.

By far, the most prevalent use of Peter – that's right, he is known as Peeing Peter in my world – is to settle one of the most crucial social issues of our time. Yes – I'm talking of the age-old question: which is better – Ford or Chevy? Peter is an equal opportunity pisser – I have seen him soaking both logos. I have seen teen-agers become involved in heated debates about which brand is better – as if the fate of the civilized world (and the larger, uncivilized world) hangs in the balance. Note to teen-agers and Peter – Have you noticed the economic plight of both car companies?

I wonder if young kids – riding in their parents' car, think "Wow – look at the kid peeing. I can't wait to get my own car, so I can have him pee on something I don't like. Maybe homework or lima beans or the clothes my parents make me wear."

It makes the world...curious. Weird. Screwed up. I don't know. There is a college football conference known as The Big Ten. It has been called that far longer than Peter has been peeing. The reason seemed to be that there were ten teams in the league. Nice – logical. Then Penn State joined to bring the total to eleven. So the new name is...The Big Ten.

Notre Dame is in Big Ten country – but it plays in the Big East. South Bend, New England. Of course, Notre Dame only plays in the Big East in some sports – not all. Certainly not football. Apparently, Notre Dame has received papal dispensation allowing them to negotiate deals unavailable to any other institution.

Of course Boston College plays in the Atlantic Coast Conference – you know – Virginia, North Carolina, Georgia Tech, et al.

College football isn't good for learning numbers or geography. But the F.A.A. is worse. They don't know colors. Every airplane has a black box. The black box is orange. But no one dares to call it the orange box. Maybe it's just a black box in orange clothing.

Someone told me I should take these things with a grain of salt. I'm not sure why. I tried a grain of salt, then sugar, and a grain of pepper, and a grain of sand. Then I tried a grain of grain. None of them helped. I was thinking of getting Peter to do his thing on various grains, but then I remembered that I hate the little pervert.

But, more important than all of this, apparently – after a year of announcements and one postponement – America was able to switch from analog TV to digital TV, and only a few million people weren't prepared. They never saw it coming, and now they may be without television until they get the appropriate converter box. I think it's a black box. I think it allows everyone in the Big Ten to see all eleven teams. I think those who weren't prepared for the big switch are the same people who adorn their vehicles with Peeing Peter.

Chapter XLV. – Hard Pressed
Or: I am Amazed

Apparently the world is full of slow learners. This is especially true of those people who, "Never cease to be amazed that..." Fill in the blank with some totally unamazing item. After twenty, or fifty, or eighty years, don't you think it's time that you finally cease to be amazed?

I'm not talking about some new, totally unexpected, miraculous occurrence, like the Cubs winning a World Series or Paris Hilton finding a cure for cancer. I'm talking about the more mundane – like the person who never ceases to be amazed that *Star Wars* movies make millions. Every single one has – and *Star Wars* volume 1,987 will also. It is no longer amazing – it's just life.

Some people are hard pressed to think of things. I am not now, nor have I ever been hard pressed – with the possible exception of one "heavy date" back in the days of my youth. The days of my youth are somewhat blurry memories now.

I've never been soft pressed, either. I'm pretty much medium pressed. Right now I'm medium impressed to figure out how drivers in Rome actually make it home alive. I recently spent two days in the Eternal City (a rather presumptuous but, thus far, accurate nickname) and I learned that American drivers aren't totally crazy – at least not when compared to Italians. There were occasions when I wanted to tremble and cry like a two-year-old instead of madly dashing across a busy intersection where I was reasonably sure that I was the fox and the Romans were the hounds.

The most popular means of transportation – and "means" is correct here – is the Kamikaze Scooter. Favored by men wearing business suits and ties, the Kamikaze Scooter splits lanes and weaves in and out of traffic with an aggression that would be envied by NASCAR drivers. Pedestrians are the speed bumps of life.

I have to admit that I did not see an accident. Actually, I don't have to admit that, but I am willing to because we have developed that kind of relationship. So I saw no accident, but at least 6,472 extremely close calls. It seems that their (the Kamikaze Scooter pilots) philosophy is, "If you haven't almost died- You're not trying!" It may be a macho thing – I'm not sure.

Only slightly less popular than the scooter was this thing called a Smart Car. You've probably seen them – on TV. They are only slightly bigger than a Fisher-Price Big Wheel, and about as helpful in an accident. But they are called Smart Cars because of their fuel efficiency and maneuverability. And because their drivers suffer some automotive form of penis envy, they get all Napoleonic about proving their manhood – by cutting off larger cars and scaring tourists. Not that they'd actually hit one – their vehicle would be destroyed.

I don't know about the name. Forget the bit about giving inanimate objects human characteristics. At least I think "smart" is a human characteristic – once-in-a-while. I'd feel a lot of pressure driving something smart. You should have to take an I.Q. test to buy one. You know there are Smart Cars being driven by dumb asses, and that seems...well...wrong...like it defeats the purpose.

Of course, Italy has bigger problems than bad drivers. Their President, Silvio Berlusconi, makes Bill Clinton look...well... certainly not like a clichéd choir boy. I don't know why choir boys are always used. He doesn't make old Bill look like a saint, either. But he sure has taken sexual scandal and infidelity to new heights... ha ha, bad choice of words...who cares? And he's seventy-two-years-old. Insert your own Viagra™ joke here. Teen-agers, prostitutes, all kinds of accusations are being made about poor Silvio. Somebody needs to buy that man a Smart Car and take him for a long ride – just watch out for Kamikaze Scooters.

Chapter XLI. – The Review
Or: The Test is Tomorrow

Let's review. When I say that in class, some teen-agers groan. That's because it often indicates a test or a paper is coming soon. Teen-agers hate tests and papers almost as much as they hate waking up before noon.

Rest assured gentle readers, you have no test or paper as a result of this review – unless it is an endurance test. In fact, you can rest unassured if you wish.

I am writing this review on July 6, 2009 at the end of one of the greatest events in my life – even greater than writing this memorable epic. As an early thirtieth wedding anniversary celebration, my wife and I went on a Mediterranean cruise. Some of you are probably thinking, "Ray's wife, Cindy, is one lucky woman." To those who may be thinking that, I say, "You are so right." To those who were not thinking that, I say, "What duh hell? Why weren't you thinking that?"

Thirty years of wedded bliss. It makes me wonder – who is Bliss and why is he involved in so many weddings? And why don't we hear about unwedded bliss more often? We know it exists.

For years I thought I would never go on a cruise, and not just for the obvious reason of cost. I always associated cruises with rich, snotty people who would be obnoxious to be with. But after taking an Alaskan cruise to celebrate our twenty-fifth anniversary of bliss, and after this one I realized…well…I guess I was absolutely right. Ha ha – LOL – I'll bet you thought I was going to say something else.

Actually, I was only partially right. There are snotty and obnoxious people – but far less than I thought. I've met lots of nice, pleasant, friendly people from all over the world. I ate dinner on the Fourth of July with a nice couple from England. It was interesting to say the least. I almost never say the least because teachers and writers have trouble with that.

But there I was with my new English friends and red, white, and blue decorations, and I didn't quite know what to say to them. I thought of, "Happy boy did you lose a great colony day," but I didn't. Or, "Happy the big one that got away day," or any number of cheeky comments, but I resisted. While we are all marveling at my restraint and good manners, let us also applaud my use of the British-oriented "cheeky." This would be a wonderful time to create your own inappropriate comment or insult.

Since none of us were around in 1776, and since our two countries are strong allies, we did the only logical thing. We sat in a bar listening to American music being sung by a man from New Zealand while drinking British beer. Somehow, that seemed appropriate.

I've also met people from countries that are not strong allies of the U.S., and guess what? They are just as nice as anyone else. Maybe world leaders should all take a cruise together.

We began in Rome, where I learned about crazy drivers and Smart Cars and Berlusconi's sexual exploits. Since then I've learned:

- Greek drivers are like Roman drivers with road rage.
- Corfu is among the most picturesque places on earth.
- Turkey is beautiful. Who knew? Maybe they need to change their name to Peacock.
- Tennessee is not the litter capitol of the world – Cairo is. Of course, Cairo has four times as many people as my entire state.
- The Nile in Cairo is not wide, is not clean, and flows through a major city. Antony and Cleopatra would weep.
- Standing in front of the pyramids and the sphinx is strangely moving, in spite of the fact that

-    The pyramids are surrounded by crooked people.

The people are not physically crooked – but they are crooks, offering camel rides for little money and then demanding more before the rider dismounts. The police – the freaking uniformed police – offer to take your picture or show you a good spot to stand and then stick their hand out demanding a tip. I thought of lots of tips, but fortunately I didn't speak Egyptian, so I did not go to jail. If I had more ambition, I would look up the Egyptian word for dickweed. I'll bet it's pronounced uniformed officer.

But the crooked people, even the cops, were not the biggest nuisance in Pyramidland. There is a flock, an entire clan of people who, even though they are nowhere near a bicycle, are called peddlers. They swarm over tourists like the paparazzi at a monthly Brangelina adoption announcement. They are more aggressive than a used car salesman on speed. They are pushing (or peddling) postcards and t-shirts and every conceivable material that can be shaped like a pyramid. Even inconceivable materials. I've been in swarms of mosquitoes that were less bothersome.

The following is a true story as overheard by your eavesdropping writer – although no eaves actually dropped, and it was easy to overhear because the parents involved were about as quiet as Dick Vitale at a Duke game. It seems that junior was not happy about going to see the camels and the desert and the pyramids. Apparently, junior would rather watch a reality show or play with his Wii (which sounds perverted).

Mom and dad were trying -- with little success – to adjust his attitude. That's when mom "brilliantly" played the historical impact card. She said, "I just want you to learn – to see where the oil we use comes from."

Junior responded, "Well, it doesn't come from camels." My wife – my eavesdropping partner – and I have had many laughs over that one.

And so we have come to the end of this class – I mean chapter – and we have reviewed nothing. I am very sorry about that. I guess the test will have to be postponed. I am easily distracted.

Chapter XLVII. – Logic 101
Or: They're Out There

The last chapter began with the words, "Let's review." Then the author got side tracked, back tracked a little, lost track of time, and Viola! No review.

Logic would indicate, or dictate, or mandate that this chapter begin with, "Let's review," followed by an actual review. Logic is over-rated – and a bit pushy. Dictate? Mandate? Who does logic think she is? And why is she female?

I would like to wrap this memorial epic up, but I'm out of wrapping paper, and people – mostly men – keep saying and doing things that make me want to write about them.

Like our state legislature for example. This robust body...wait – what exactly is a robust body? Does it have anything to do with Sheryl Crow? Anyway, thanks to our legislature, people in the state of Tennessee can, for the first time ever, carry concealed weapons in our state parks. I'm not sure what pressing need prompted this change, but whatever it was, change has taken place. What is the opposite of a pressing need? After guaranteeing our right to keep our arms unbared in parks where children play, our congress people were not satisfied. They needed one more place to let pistol-packin' mamas and papas pack their pistols. (This is not a reference to the singing group called the Mamas and the Papas, although *Monday, Monday* is now playing in my brain). So our congress people thought short and soft. They suggested churches and schools and shopping malls before finally settling on the absolute ideal place for guns to be. They picked bars and restaurants.

That's right, after a century or two of people eating and drinking unarmed, people in the Volunteer State can now drink while carrying a weapon, because alcohol and firearms are a perfect combination.

I know some will view my complaint here as liberal, anti-gun, get more government in our lives kind of rhetoric. To those people, I say, "Stick 'em up." Ha ha. Okay, lower your hands. I know about the Second Amendment. I own guns. I used to hunt. I know you have to have a permit to carry a concealed weapon. But I also know that, with all the problems facing our state, addressing the lack of firearms in bars is...well...amazing.

But why stop there? If you can't beat 'em, join 'em. (That's an original cliché I just made up). Why not combine the gun shops and the bars – sort of one-stop shopping at its finest. Let every gun shop have a liquor license. Let every bar sell guns. Think of the great names these establishments can have, like:

Whiskey and Weapons
Rum and Rifles
Pinot and Pistols
And my personal favorite, *Ouzo and Uzis.* Also:
Bourbon and Bullets
Vodka and Violence
Margaritas and Mayhem

It's a natural. The word magnum is used with wine and guns. A shooter can be a drink or a person firing a weapon. Yup – we can take the shotgun approach to handle things in a rapid-fire sort of way. Guns and guzzling never sounded better. Someone orders another round, he might mean drinks or ammo. When a man tries, unsuccessfully, to pick up a woman in a bar he is shot down. Don't think I'd use that term if I were in *Whiskey and Weapons.* Wouldn't want to be fired from there either. Before long, the bars will have swinging doors and Marshall Dillon and Miss Kitty will be there, and we will call it progress – or getting back to our traditional values. And I can think of more than twenty tacky things to say about the name Miss Kitty, but I won't.

I cannot conclude this book until I make my big announcement. You didn't know about the big announcement? Well, now you do. While cruising the Mediterranean, I made a huge discovery –a monumental discovery that must be shared. I am going to do that, but not in this chapter. In the literary world, this is called building suspense. In the non-literary world, it is called being obnoxious. I am glad I am in the literary world.

So be patient, wait for the huge announcement, and have a round on me. PULL!

Chapter XLVIII. – Taxing Times
Or: What's Cooking?

Sometimes our state legislators get it right. Next week we will hold our annual, "Back to School Tax Free Weekend." It wasn't an original idea with our congress people – other states had done it for years. But we do it, also.

The idea is to give people some financial relief from one of the highest sales taxes in America. Coupled with traditional, "Back to School Sales," people can save a decent amount of money – at least they can if they spend lots of money. There is no telling how much would have to be spent to save an indecent amount of money.

The items that are tax exempt include clothes, notebooks and other school supplies, and computers. That's it. I think it is a wonderful start, but why stop there? Going back to school involves much more than clothes and supplies and computers.

First of all, there is food. Taxing food is a little mean anyway, but how are our students expected to survive without gum and candy and energy drinks and junk food? How are we going to maintain our obesity rates without a little tax relief? Come on congress people.

If there is one area that absolutely, positively, no possible doubt about it qualifies as a school necessity, it would be make-up. How in the hell can most females and some males even consider returning to the hallowed halls of academia without a major financial investment in make-up? The halls where I teach aren't really hallowed – except at Halloween – but that doesn't matter. Back to school make-up should be tax free. And all items known as toiletries. If you have even taught in a confined area with deodorantless freshmen boys, you understand.

The computer should not be the only tax-free electronic device. Back to school cell phones that will be confiscated by school officials should be tax free. So should back to school iPods™. Or earPods.

It is possible that some would be offended if I suggested a tax free, back to school condom sale, so I won't suggest it – even though Tennessee ranks fourth in the country in teen-age pregnancy. I would not want to be accused of encouraging those pesky teen-agers to engage in sexual behavior. Just say no pesky teen-agers.

Spoiled rich kids should be allowed to purchase tax free back to school vehicles to flaunt at the poor kids. Teachers should be allowed to purchase a year's supply of aspirin and alcohol tax free. I'll bet my astute readers can think of many other items as well. I think everyone should make a list and then call his or her congress person and demand action.

Speaking of Mediterranean cruises, I must say that I truly miss being on that cruise. I absolutely must say it. I miss seeing new and beautiful places, meeting new people, and eating fine foods. I don't feel pampered anymore. In fact, I now have to place my own napkin on my lap. That's right, non-cruisers. Fancy schmancy establishments have the waiter or waitress place your napkin on your lap so that you don't have to be bothered or inconvenienced by such a difficult chore.

I don't like the term waiter. It seems to me that once I order my food, I'm the one doing the waiting. Server is a better term, but it sounds like something related to tennis. I'm also not crazy about having my napkin placed on my lap by a complete, or even a partial stranger. It seems like an invasion of a significant space.

I'm also not sure about the word chef. I don't know how that came about. I think a chef is a cook with a bigger hat.

But I am sure that – because of this cruise – I discovered something so significant that it will be the subject of a major announcement. And that major announcement is...coming soon. I will make it after I get through buying my tax free back to school items. I think napkins should be on that list.

Chapter XLVIX. –
The Penultimate Chapter
Or: It's a Wrap (Almost)

Let's review. No, really. I know I've said that before, but I really mean it this time. No distractions or changing the subject.

The thing about health care reform is…Just kidding. I don't want to talk about health care reform. It's too complicated. I'd rather talk about music. I love music. And since I need to review and wrap this up, I'm going to use wrap music.

I was going to be real cleaver here and write a little rap song, but I feared it would be another one of those, "White guy tries to be cool and proves he's got no game" moments, so I won't. So you don't get to experience the following:

I'm sittin' in my crib
Wonderin' what to do
I need to find a way
To do my review
Wrappin' up my book
Is takin' too long
I ain't got no time
For this silly wrap song

So let's review. My closest and dearest friend Sheryl wrote the following lyrics:

I don't have digital
I don't have Diddly Squat

That sent me on a quest to find Diddly Squat. It was a quest fraught with peril. It was not just full of peril, it was fraught with it. You might want to use the word fraught the next time you think someone is full of something. You sir, or madam, are fraught with shit. But I digress.

The quest for Diddly Squat took us (because we travelled together) through the land of the Curmudgeon Virgins, into the Valley of the GameDay crew, and beyond the universe of those gallant Mall Walkers. We battled dickweeds and learned to think in the box. We explored Facebook and the scintillating world of teenagers. We went from mullets to the joys of flying – in a plane that is. And like all quests, we returned home wiser for the experience.

I have written other books. In fact, there are three novels that I am going to shamelessly mention now. The first is *Picking Up Jellyfish (Or: The Bobble Head Legacy)*. The second is *Guitars and Telescopes*. The third is *No New Messages*. They are works of fiction. This is my first word of art. Ha ha ha – LOL – I mean my first work of non-fiction.

Sometimes people ask how long it takes to write a book. For this one, I believe the correct answer is fifty-seven years, although that isn't the answer people are looking for. Usually it takes about nine months, just like most full term deliveries (although this labor is <u>much</u> easier).

I began in the fall of 2008. It is now the summer of 2009. Two people mentioned in this book (Walter Cronkite and Billy Mayes) have died. We know who the new president is. School will start soon, followed by college football, and even though there STILL isn't a playoff, at least there is the joy and hope and enthusiasm of a new season. And it's like coming full circle – although no one ever comes partial circle – and all is right with the world.

So this would probably be a great time to make the major announcement I have been promising. Drums begin to roll –

trumpets prepare to blare. Here it is. This summer, while cruising the Mediterranean, I actually discovered the identity of Diddly Squat. It was like something out of a morality play. I wasn't really looking for him – and that's when I found him. In Egypt. Which brings me to another major announcement. In the next chapter, I will reveal his identity.

Chapter L. – Grand Finale
Or: How Cool Is It That

I Have Exactly Fifty Chapters-
and How Long Can I Make This
Subtitle Before People Stop
Reading It – and What Would
Happen If the Chapter Subtitle
Is Longer Than the Actual
Chapter?

Picture the Sahara Desert. Wait – don't picture it yet. In the Egyptian language, the word Sahara means desert. So when we say the Sahara Desert, we are actually saying the desert desert. I'll bet many Egyptians have had a hearty chuckle over that one. What's with the body parts and laughter? Hearty chuckles and belly laughs and splitting a gut laughing.

Picture the desert desert. Heat waves shimmer in the distance. Sometimes they shimmy and shake and do the Watusi – but today, they are just shimmering. The great Pyramids of Giza rise before us. Camels are squatting – hissing and spitting and stinking in the hot sun. One camel is named Clyde – after the Ray Stevens' song. If you don't know *Ahab the A-Rab* and his camel named Clyde, well... you might as well keep going now because this is the last chapter. Another camel is named...

I'm not going to do the other names. I was going to make up some tacky political/camel references – like the camel who wouldn't stop running and the one that quit before her term – I mean trip – was finished, but I changed my mind. I'm trying to reach closure here, and I'm wondering why we never hear about openure, and I fear that the ending is predictable. A camel named Diddly, squatting in the sun would, in fact, be predictable.

But an Egyptian cop in a white uniform with a machine gun slung over his back like a rock singer's guitar would not be predictable, would it?

Unfortunately, it was the camel. I didn't get close enough to the cops to learn any names, and I wouldn't want to offend them in case they read this. I'm thinking that this book might be a big hit in Egypt, so I'm going to use the camel.

So there it is. We set out *In Search of Diddly Squat* and found Diddly the Camel Squatting by the Pyramids. What a journey. Now you know Diddly – although you may not be able to actually have Diddly. But as my special and remarkable friend Sheryl would say:

It's not having what you want
It's wanting what you've got

And I, like my gentle and ungentle readers, have much to be thankful for. I am thankful that Sheryl will soon be reading this and, no doubt, want to meet me. I am sure I will end up on Oprah – the show, not the person. So life is good. I think I'll *Soak up the Sun.*

/